A BUTTERFLY WITH BURNING WINGS

~Novel~

Corinne Wandenburg

For my dear good friend Liping Wang, who is far away from me. I hope to see you someday! With all my love, Corinne!

Infarom Publishing

office@infarom.com
www.infarom.com

ISBN: 978-973-1991-65-8

Publisher: **INFAROM**
Author: **Corinne Wandenburg**
Translator: **Maria Letiția Chiculiță**
Correction editor: **CarolAnn Johnson**
Cover design: **Liping Wang**
Original title: *Un fluture cu aripile arse* (Romanian)

PROLOGUE

It has always been more difficult for me to write letters; it has seemed easier to me to tell a person directly, face to face, what I have to say. Thoughts laid down on paper seem if not false – which is not representative of me – at least somehow different than if they had been spoken. I believe it is easier to get rid of someone by writing to that person than by saying to his or her face what you have to say. If you lie to the person standing in front of you, you are covered in most cases, especially if that person does not reply, whereas in a dialogue there is a sometimes certain awkwardness in a lie, which writing suppresses most of the time.

The story that I hope you will enjoy in the upcoming pages is the story of a woman who went through life striking against everything that stood in her way. It is also my story because she and I grew up together, and then later on, I followed her through her bleak destiny for which she had had such high hopes. I followed her to heal my soul, and she followed her path hoping for joy and happiness, which she never achieved. And yet these difficulties did not hold her down; on the contrary, they made her stronger through her almost annoying silence and the prayers she uttered to the Heavenly Father under the scrutiny of her hostile companions. This is how her youth and adulthood passed, while she yearned for her country and her dear family.

When she became a Queen, our relationship did not change at all. I remained her friend, and soon after her marriage, when depression gradually surrounded her like a fog, making her ill-tempered, I was there by her side and we cried on each other's shoulders, disregarding the fact that she was a Queen and I was merely her companion. We were truly friends; we were inseparable. No one ever filled my spot in her heart, and I

3

am gratified by that. She is gone now, but I live to write about her and the kindness that lighted her soul.

So I will tell you the story of a true lady, whom I followed all her life, and whom I accompanied, after years spent among strangers, back to the house where she was born,. Many things happened before that redeeming year of 1692. To me, Catarina de Braganza is the most noble being that Portugal gave at that time. Her strong blood and her prayers helped her overcome all the humiliations she endured while holding her head high in that country of heretics. Loneliness bonded us even closer when her husband, Charles II, was dying, and called for her, but she refused to see him.

We were each other's shield when the crowds were shouting against our religion; we suffered together when she miscarried children, when the world and Parliament demanded divorce, but especially when his mistresses would come and go from her husband's bed, defying her with an "army" of acknowledged bastards, even from the very beginning of their marriage.

We were a bit more relaxed when, following her husband, his Catholic brother took the throne, but our illusions vanished like lightning. Later, we went back home to Portugal together, two old ladies whose stubborn spirit alone kept us alive and standing. I did see the graves of my family, but she would never see England and the grave of her husband again.

Our cabins on the ship were next to one another, so that I could hear perfectly when she knocked on the thin wall. People in England treated us with a restrained deference, clearly letting us know that they were glad we were leaving the country where we had spent so many years. At that time, Catarina was 54 and I was 51. She was wearing black clothing, although our souls were happy to return to our country. If she had ever been beautiful, you would have not known it at that moment, but her eyes were just as young as ever. Unfortunately, in England's court, she was not considered such a beautiful woman, but that is not how I saw her. She was beautiful like a Portuguese woman, with a dark complexion, tall, raised in a mild climate. She could not be compared to any other lady on the island, where the rain, the humidity, and the cold made it necessary to burn a lot of wood.

Once, she invited me to visit her in her cabin. When she saw me enter the room, she smiled and invited me to have a light breakfast prepared by her faithful maid and servant Marisa, who had been her by her side, just as I had, since 1662. The rest of the servants had died or left the good Queen Catarina.

4

The Queen was wearing a simple black dress, and her only jewelry was a golden cross she had had since she was a child, set on a thick chain that her mother – God rest her soul! – had given her. On her head, she had an arrangement of black lace caught in her gray hair with a simple jewel. She had taken almost all of the jewels she had brought with her to England in 1662 – they were all gifts from her parents – and she was wearing a ring on each hand. I remember how I waited impatiently for the ship to leave the harbor to sail from Portsmouth to Lisbon. When the boat slowly weighed anchor and moved, Catarina uttered a cry and came out of her cabin. On the deck, I caught her standing still, her face toward the city that had received her full of hope back in 1662. She did not cry, but I did see something – regret? – blended with hatred, for her life had just passed by pathetically in those lands. I also saw hope in her eyes, hope for a better life, there where we were heading, where the crew and the ship were taking us. This was an English ship that Mary II had made available for us. Catarina's brother, Pedro II, was waiting for us, his arms wide open; she had been secretly writing to him before this conclusive, definitive departure to her parents' Kingdom. It hurt her that she had to ask for permission to leave England, but Mary II let her go with obvious relief.

I heard her say then to me, on the deck, that we were going back home, that we had stayed away from our country for too long; then she took one last look at the city that was growing dimmer and dimmer, and we entered the cabin where Marisa had gathered the remains from our frugal breakfast, leaving only the tea and the biscuits.

My Queen had always loved biscuits....

So follow us, if we have made you curious!

Juliana de Alfambra, the elder daughter of Earl of Alfambra

CHAPTER 1

My dear Catarina was born on the 25th of November, 1638, as the second daughter of the Duke of Braganza Joao and his wife Luiza, in the famous house of the Dukes of Medina Sidonia, subsequently fallen when Portugal split from Spain, and Joao became King of his country under the name of Joao IV.

My father was a very good friend of her father, so we grew up together; her being a King's daughter did not matter to us. I was in the Royal Palace most of the time, and Catarina had assumed the role of a sort of mother to me. She protected me, for I was smaller; she made me laugh, and I wanted to be with her all the time. It was difficult for me to be apart from her, and I believe she would have said the same thing about me. When we both got older, I would stay overnight at their house, which made us both very happy. We were two quiet girls, raised somehow far from the glamor and pomp of the court that Joana, the elder sister of Catarina, began to understand and watch from a hidden corner at a ball, unseen by anybody. We did not play with her very often; she was different from us. She was bored easily, and especially since she was older than we, she did not take our games seriously. The Princess of Beira was a dreamer. She was waiting to grow up, to wear long dresses and beautiful jewels and dance until morning, which did not impress me or her sister at all. She was six years older than I and three years older than Catarina.

I don't know much about the boys in the family, who were few, anyway. We never played with Alfonso, for he was a strange-tempered child. Teodosio seemed to be too old for us and full of the importance of the title he carried, which his father impressed upon him. Pedro was too small, even for me, and I don't really know what to say about his

6

childhood. This may be also because in 1651, Catarina and I went to the monastery to complete our education, religious training, and manners – she with a view to marrying a prince, and I with hopes to marry the son of a duke or some similarly titled suitor, appropriate to my father's social status. I was ten back then, and Catarina was thirteen. We did not want to be separated, and the nuns and the Queen agreed not to break up this friendship. Who knows what was in the Queen's mind, what her thoughts were back then? Was she thinking that I would be her daughter's Lady of Honor ten years from then? Nobody could foretell that, but we were quite happy together, even if a Catholic monastery overcomes, through decency and severity, any capricious thought. My father was thrilled about this decision for me to accompany a princess; he was honored. I would come home only for Christmas and Easter, for a month each time.

For the nuns, I was raw material only waiting to be molded. As years went by, the foolishness, the friskiness passed, and a certain dignity took hold of us as our manners improved; when the princess passed her sixteenth birthday, her mother came to see her very often, as she had started to supervise her education even more. We were living in the same large room in the monastery, so we knew when she would come. There were also other girls there, but we did not often associate with them. We had our own path to walk, as well as our dedicated mothers watching over us.

When the *Infanta* turned eighteen, she was informed that we would soon leave the monastery to get to know also the secrets of the world, not just the ones of God. I remember as if it were yesterday how much we cried. We thought we would be separated soon, with her married God knows where, and me left in Lisbon, entering a marriage and expecting letters that no one would ever send me. I lived a troubling and tiring existence during those two remaining months we spent in the monastery after that time. When I turned sixteen, in January of 1657, I was not exactly happy, for I knew that in early February we would leave; she would go to the royal palace while I would return to my father's house. All we could do was pray. We could still send each other notes, we could still see each other, but we no longer shared the same room. We had to let go of each other and hope that we would both be married soon.

The day we left the monastery in different carriages, Catarina accompanied by the guards of her father and I in my father's carriage with his emblem, we both cried, waving our handkerchiefs until our roads parted, each going in a different direction.

Catarina had remained the only girl in the family. There were three children left out of five. Teodosio and Joana had passed away that same

7

year, 1653. I remember not having attended the funeral. Alfonso was just as strange as ever, and he would have an outbreak of madness every now and then, which would frighten Catarina, especially in her first months at home. Only Pedro, an eight-year-old boy, was her joy. She loved playing with him, but not for too long, because they all believed he should not be influenced by a woman and that a woman should not trouble him too much. He was the hope to the throne of Portugal and his brother was very much aware of that.

When we were allowed to see each other, I noticed gladly that Catarina's attitude toward me was unchanged. She just had to be more reserved, more restrained in public, but when we were all alone, our feelings toward each other would come out as ever.

The next year, when she turned twenty, Catarina had to choose a Lady of Honor, and with the consent of her parents she chose me. Thus, on Christmas in 1658, I settled in a small apartment next to my friend's. In three weeks, I would turn eighteen, and I was to make my appearance with all the splendour at my first ball. My father, the Earl, was pleased, and my mother had very carefully chosen my jewels and dresses. My being so close to the royal family gave them and my brothers high hopes for some brilliant marriages. I lived with Catarina until May of 1662, one next to the other; I always found her to be the same girl I grew up with at the monastery. We didn't go out of the palace often. Luiza, Catarina's mother, was afraid for our safety, which is why I can count on my fingers the number of times we went for a walk. And yet, we did not lack freedom; we had less of that at the monastery, and also there were no balls there.

I knew that they wanted the princess to get married, so they held many balls, and the two of us were the pure expression of astonishment and joy brought together. We were beautiful, young, full of life; Catarina was taller, while I was smaller, and took everything as if it were all a game until I fell in love. It truly came, it truly struck me, and I have never felt again what I felt then. Catarina was unconcerned; she knew that her mother was planning with the Stuarts to marry her to Charles. It was all the same to her. But what about me? She had not even seen her husband-to-be, but I had seen my chosen one – at a ball, of course. They were celebrating the signing of the agreement for the marriage of Catarina to Charles II of England. My friend was about to become a Queen and go far away. How can I say this? My feelings were bittersweet during that time. Catarina had the habit of entering my room all of a sudden, and thus, she caught me crying. I told her everything. I was in love with her cousin, and I thought he liked me, too. Her cousin, Gaspar Juan Pérez de Guzmán, the future Earl X of Medina Sidonia, was the one who stole my heart, but he was

8

caught up in the net of his wife, Antonia. He had no children, much to his sadness. Catarina came to calm me down, to comfort me with the idea that all must be forgotten, that marriage to her cousin was impossible. Who would have dissolved his first one?

"You will come with me to England, Juliana, and you will be my Lady of Honor. You will forget him," said the princess, wiping my tears with her own handkerchief, "but first I will do something for you. You will meet him in secrecy, in my apartment. I shall stay in the boudoir, and you two will have a polite conversation, and you will explain things to each other. One single meeting, and then you must forget about him! You know he will return to Spain; he is not welcome here."

I kissed her hands and agreed to that plan. What else could I have done? Maybe he was unhappy, too; maybe he did not love his wife. Actually, that was the truth, which I was to learn soon. When Marisa, the *Infanta*'s young maid discretely slipped a note to Gaspar in his pocket, he was very surprised seeing that the note was from his cousin and that he was supposed to come to her apartment, which he did immediately. There he found me and not his next of kin, which came as a surprise to him, but then seeing my tears, he understood.

He came near the chair where I was sitting, so excited, and he kissed my hand, without letting it go afterwards. I did not have the power to withdraw it. Our eyes silently spoke a thousand words. Then Gaspar told me that he did not love Antonia, that he was unhappy, that he did not have a heir, and that his wife had been a bad but necessary choice at its time. He also told me that he had fallen in love with me from the moment our eyes first met in the ballroom. My answer was much the same. Then we talked about my plan to go to England with his cousin, never to return. I also told him my decision not to get married and to have only him in my heart forever. Gaspar was to leave for Spain a few days later, so we each went on our separate paths in life. I had given him, I still remember as if it were yesterday, what I had prepared before our meeting, namely a lock of my hair hidden in the medallion I wore around my neck. He kissed it and asked me to help him fasten it around his neck. He hid it directly on his skin, next to his heart, then he kissed my hands, which trembled at his touch. He thought of what to give me and he took his ring from his right ring finger. This was a ring with his earl's coat of arms, and his initials were engraved inside it.

My tears fell in streams, and he dared to take me in his arms. I completely forgot where I was; I forgot about my friend hidden in the boudoir. I was living in my short dream, which would have to be enough for me for the rest of my life, when the swish of a dress made us look up. Catarina, tears in her eyes, was there by our side, looking at us.

"Go, Gaspar, go, please! May God watch you! Juliana will always love you; you can see that, and you can feel it, too. You shall never see her again. You two must separate now and say farewell to each other. Yes, so soon and so abruptly! Just kiss her and go, quickly! Maybe someone is already missing you." That was, of course, an allusion to his wife.

Gaspar and I joined our lips with bitter tears. The kiss was so brief, and yet so intense, as if all our thoughts had been gathered into that pleasant but so painful touch. He kissed my hand one more time, and with his face toward me, he backed out of the room, stumbling. One more second and his face was gone forever, but I had the ring. I had something to hold onto. I sank into the armchair, my hands on my face, and cried a river, kissing the ring of my dear Gaspar. Catarina was standing next to me, also crying.

"I wonder what the future has in store for me, Juliana. I sense that it is nothing good. I don't know why I have the feeling that this marriage is going to be a disaster. I'm thinking, though, that you will be there by my side and that I will cry on your shoulder, as you are crying on mine now."

I consented to that, wiping my tears and trying to come back to my senses. There was still a long way to go until then, until the departure from our country. There were still ceremonies during which I had to appear happy and smiling. I asked for the princess's permission to go to my house. I had to find a golden chain to put my lover's ring on. It would stay there next to my heart forever. It is still there now. I shall never be apart from it.

Indeed, I have never seen Gaspar again since then. The following year, when the *Infanta* married in absentia, in Lisbon, he did not attend the reception, and it was better that way. Immediately after that, the preparations began for the real departure and for the true ceremony in England with her husband next to her. Catarina was already Queen of England; she was "Catherine" then. But I was to act the same way toward her; I only had to be more reserved in public. The servants had already started packing up things, and we had nothing else to do but wait. My mother came often to see me. She brought me the jewels to take with me, and the villa where I was born was now rightfully mine. Were I to return to Portugal, I had a deed showing I owned that house. My brothers did not oppose it – on the contrary, they were very conveniently married, maybe also thanks to me. My father, the Earl, let my mother do whatever she pleased, so he did not object. That gesture relieved me; it was like a refuge, even though useless to me then.

Thus the days went by, and the moment of our having to embark came as if unexpectedly. Everything was loaded on the deck of a Portuguese ship led by a cheerful and honored captain who was always smiling. I had just met him on our departure day. I was anxious to leave. The waiting was nagging at me, especially since everybody congratulated me on my sudden good fortune, while I felt miserable because I was leaving my town, my country, and my family, not to mention that poor soul in Spain, close to Cadiz, of whom only God knew how he was doing and how unhappy he was. Catarina was my consolation.

CHAPTER 2

As I said before, I never saw Gaspar again, even though deep down in my heart, I just hoped, like a child, that I would yet find him there in the harbor, seeing us before leaving. I was like a silly girl incurably in love. I remember how I got on board with the highest honors, how we kissed the royal family and my family goodbye. I remained outside on the deck until the ship was about to leave; suddenly a man came upstairs onto the bridge toward me and Catarina, then knelt down. When he was ordered to get up, he handed me an envelope, then vanished from sight. The envelope was for me, and it was from the person I wanted it so much to come from. I could tell when I saw the coat of arms of the Medina Sidonia family. I quickly hid the envelope in my bosom; even though the people on the shore saw that, they could no longer ask for explanations.

The bridge had been lifted, and the ship could leave at any given time. We waved our hands and handkerchiefs until we got tired. The Regent Luiza and her brother Pedro smiled at Catarina and blew her kisses from a distance. Alfonso VI, then King under his mother's auspices, was laughing insanely. That he was a lunatic was plain to see. He was standing next to his friend, the Count of Castelo Melhor, the King's only friend, especially in evildoing. Alphonse started laughing and tormenting more and more noisily until he swerved and was on the verge of falling. The two servants tasked with looking after him took him by the arms much to his despair. Screaming maliciously, he was taken to the carriage, accompanied by the malevolent count, his good friend. It was difficult for Catarina to see her brother like that.

"This is a bad sign, Juliana, I can feel it!" she told me during those moments.

After the sunny shore of Portugal receded from view, we entered the cabin made ready for the Queen of England. I took the letter out of my bosom, and when I opened it, a lock of my sweetheart's hair fell on my lap. I immediately placed it in a medallion next to the ring I had received before. In that sad letter, he was pouring out his love, saying that the chain on his neck was kissed like a precious jewel at every possible moment. He told me about the disgrace the Duke's house had fallen into, about Antonia's malice, and the miserable life he was living. Catarina was listening to all of that calmly, then she frowned, telling me the news she had learned in different ways about her husband. He was a womanizer; he had had many mistresses, and rumor had it that he also had children born out of wedlock. We were wondering what that marriage would be like, what Catarina's role would be in a hostile country whose language she had not mastered. We also learned that she was not wanted, for she was Catholic, but that her wedding dowry was generous enough for them to close their eyes to her catholicism. Also, she was considered old to be a bride as she would soon turn 24, in November. No matter how we might have interpreted these things, her foreboding made her shiver. Prayers did not help her calm down – on the contrary, she was wondering whether she would be allowed to be a Catholic, especially since two priests of the Holy Church were accompanying us, and our servants practiced the same religion.

Thus, the Queen, my dear friend, foresaw the miserable destiny awaiting her. She also saw that fate in the eyes of the mad King Alfonso, whose picture persisted in her mind. It is true that I did not envy her anything; I knew I would be looked upon with the same hostility. I tried to distract her thoughts toward dresses, linings, jewels, but the topic came back obsessively. Everything stood as an omen. I had a consolation: the letter and the lock of hair from Gaspar. Nobody was waiting for me at England's doors, and I had something to kiss every night until my departure from this world. The ring and the medallion were there at my neck. I could feel their warmth next to my heart, and I was thinking that he too would wear my jewel until death.

The ship we were traveling in was fancy, fastuous, and full of the luxury a princess – actually a Queen – was supposed to be surrounded with. It was beautifully built, and Marisa and I had our cabins next to those of Catarina, yet separated from the cabins of the noblemen who accompanied us. Guards watched our cabins as if we had been on land at the palace. The uniforms of the sailors bore the coat of arms of the Braganza House, sewed with golden thread; everything shone with cleanliness and the atmosphere was one of expectation, contrasting with

Catarina's feelings, which were foreboding. One could tell that she was longing for her family, for the places where we used to walk so many times. Her English teacher bored her terribly, and she preferred daydreaming. There was only water all around us, and the waves were gently caressing the ship, which sailed forward irreversibly. Many of those accompanying us would return on the same boat after the ceremony, but there were also families that decided to stay by the Queen's side and make up a sort of small Portuguese Court within the larger Court of England.

We were all Catholic, and every day we attended the Mass held by our two priests. That hour calmed us profoundly, and it felt as if our prayers reinforced our souls for what was to come. We filled our thoughts with hope, praying that God would be there with us, on our side, more than before. During the monotonous evenings, we were thinking, alone in our cabins, about our parents and siblings left there on the shore in our dear Lisbon, where people were warm like the weather, about the churches and monasteries where we would always enter hesitantly, without making any sound, about the nuns' smiles and the swish of their simple and austere clothes. In our souls, we would take everything with us to England, our beloved Portugal that we had gained back from the Spanish more than twenty years before. Gaspar was Spanish, too, but I didn't care. I just knew I would never fall in love again, nor would I change my religion by marrying some Anglican English man having principles different from mine. I was going to be all alone, serving only Catarina, and praying for my sweetheart, my beloved one, married in Spain. I knew that nothing bound him to Antonia. He was no longer in love with her; they had no children. They were married, indeed, but they did not fulfill their duties as husband and wife. He wrote to me about that also in that letter that I so fortuitously received upon embarkment, and I believed him with all my heart.

At last, one day early in the morning, the captain knocked at my cabin door, letting me know that we could see England's shore through the spyglass. We would soon be landing, only a couple of hours later. This is the news I took to Catarina. She was not sleeping, but reading a book. I only told her this much:

"Catarina, it's time! It's time we dressed you in your royal clothes."

I remember her laying her book aside and getting up, sighing, telling me she was ready. The preparations took two hours to accomplish, which did not leave me much time to get dressed, but my handy servant worked it all out perfectly. I was going to be presented with my father's

14

title, namely Countess of Alfambra, Lady of Honor, and so forth. Catarina and I wore heavy garments made of expensive materials, sewed with golden and silver threads. Our hair had been done as if for an important ceremony. Catarina was excited about her jewels; I wore only the long chain around my neck where my soul and heart were suspended, and which I could hide in my corset. I had a small diadem on my head, and matching earrings, all given by my mother upon my leaving. Catarina wore a heavy tiara on an intricate hairdo; her dress was burgundy, and it fell very well on her tall body. I chose a gray dress for the ceremony related to our entering England.

We were both tired and anxious to set foot on the ground, to get some rest in a bed that didn't swing with us, but remained motionless. We ate a bit; it was evident that we were overwhelmed by emotions. Marisa set everything around us, for we were incapable of doing much of anything in that mood. When we finally came near Portsmouth, the captain called us outside where the guards and our nobles were already waiting for us. A huge carpet had been laid down. Everybody was saluting us, waiting for us to land. I remained in the middle of the group, next to Catarina who ordered me to stay close to her under any circumstances.

"It doesn't look like it's raining," she said. "And I believe people are waiting for us! Let's see who exactly," she added, handing me the spyglass, to have a look for myself.

There was indeed a crowd in the harbor, but we did not know whether the King would be there, too. We would come to learn that soon. The disappointment we had! When we came ashore, he was nowhere to be found. All kinds of officials welcomed their Queen, some of them smiling, others whispering, others displaying barely concealed hostility. There was also a guard who, together with our officers, made up the vanguard of the convoy to the palace where we were taken, all of those on board, without many acclamations or obvious joy. The carriages were well appointed, especially the one I and the Queen of that hostile people boarded. When we reached our destination, everything was very welcoming and beautifully set. Our apartments were next to one other with a door between them through which we could communicate. Thus, we were not separated, not even for a few seconds. It was May 13, 1662. When I came through our common door, Catarina was reading a letter she had found on her bed.

"It is from Charles," she told me, continuing to read it.

When she finished reading, she threw it on the bed as if it were some kind of distasteful creature. She asked me to read it, and I immediately understood her dismay. Charles was welcoming her; he hoped she would enjoy England, but he did not know when he would arrive to take his bride. He also said that they would marry in that coastal city and that he would agree to a Catholic ceremony, in secrecy, besides the official Anglican one. Catarina began to cry, just thinking how insignificant she was, left there and greeted that way. She wondered how long she would have to wait for him, especially since his attitude was completely offensive.

Her presentiments came true. Her brother, the King, had had good reason to laugh when we left. Mad people always tell the truth in their gestures. During dinner that night, the Queen did not display anything of what was burning her soul ever since we came to Portugal. She had asked the peers we travelled with on the ship not to show themselves outraged, for that was a situation they had to endure, since she was already the Queen of England. The contracts had been signed a long time ago, so Charles probably did not consider it necessary for him to show up as well. They had been married since April, even if not at the Church, no matter what that church might have been. One week later, we hed become accustomed to this abandonment. We walked in the alleys behind the palace, weather permitting; we were taking the odious English lessons, which I hated even more since we had been living in the city.

Charles finally arrived, when Catarina's nerves were on the verge of shattering. He was a tall man, fit for our Queen, for she was tall, too, unlike me, who was shorter. He knew how to approach and address women. He was gallant; he knew how to talk and how to make himself liked by everyone. He studied me at length, annoyingly, to what end I do not know; should he have ever wanted to seduce me, that never happened. This is precisely why his shabby behavior and rude conduct disgusted his wife from the very first moment. She had been raised in a different way and she would have not appreciated "sugariness," as they put it. They immediately got married. That palace was the witness of the secret Catholic ceremony for which we had waited so long. The rest of the world witnessed a show of the Anglican ceremony, much of which the Queen did not understand. She had uttered her vows of faith to her husband in English with difficulty. He was very kind and tolerant; one could see that he had long studied my friend, and that her charms were not enough to keep him next to her, or better said, in her bedroom. Catarina didn't want that; I saw that she was impatient to see it all end and for us go to London so we could finally settle down and not have to stay any more in strange foreign places with people of icy politeness who would barely bow before

16

their Queen; it was obvious that she mattered only for the acquisition of Tangier and Bombay, as well as for the previously sent dowry.

The crowd cheered them as they left the church, but standing in the back, I could hear many people saying she was a bit too dark and too dull, if not even old. They seemed a nice couple to me: they were both tall, he was pale, while she had a bit darker complexion. There was a moment when they both smiled, and the English cheered even more. After I helped her get in the carriage, they were both left alone. On our way to London, I was in a different carriage, together with the two Catholic priests accompanying us, who were openly dissatisfied, but who said nothing, though they probably did later when they were alone. Half of the Portuguese noblemen had gone back to the palace where they had been accommodated for a week to wait for the return of the ship in which we had all arrived. In our group were almost twenty noblemen, as well as the servants and the priests, so all together we were around thirty Portuguese on that English island.

The entourage had to go about seventy-five miles to London. I was very curious, and I spent the whole time looking out of the carriage window. We passed through all kinds of villages and cities where people would bow before the King's carriage, as the Queen waved at them with a slight smile; then the crowd cheered even more. We were accompanied by the royal guards who made room for us to pass, and thus we moved forward more easily toward London. I knew that trip would soon end, and that my apartment was on the same floor as the Queen's. My apartment was not next to hers – Charles had the apartment next to hers, as was only natural, but still I was close by. I had asked Catarina, and she had asked Charles in return, who said that everything was appropriately arranged for her Portuguese Lady of Honor. The emphasizing of my Portuguese origin bothered me, as if I had come from a different world, a world less evolved than the English one.

When we reached the palace, the whole Court was gathered, and the reception was truly royal. Among the noblemen, there were some who had the same religion as we did, which gave us hope for our peace and tranquility, mine and my Queen's. We took our leave soon that night as we were all tired. I liked the apartment they had reserved for me; it was tastefully appointed, and I was waited upon by a quite kind and polite maid who was to serve me, in addition to my personal maid. Marisa was with her mistress, and probably she had other maids as well. Catarina did not go to sleep before she saw and hugged me. She was a bit scared of what awaited her, for she knew she was supposed to wait for her husband. I encouraged her, and I left a bit more at peace.

17

I wasn't expecting anyone, and I did not hold any plans in that respect. Gaspar was my whole heart. There was no room left for anyone else. So I prayed, then I kissed the jewels I wore at my neck and went to bed, giving in to the sleep overtaking me.

There I was in my new home. Night passed quickly, and I woke up when rain started pelting the windows. That persistent dampness I was to hate for the whole duration of my stay there on the island. I sat upright when I heard the door squeaking and saw it opening apparently by itself. It was the Queen. She came toward me and held out her hands for me. Then she sat down beside me on the bed, and by her looks, she did not sleep all night long.

"Charles left me right after the wedding, but not to sleep, instead to go to some mistress of his. I don't think that he likes me, I don't think I matter much to him. I shall have the fate of his cousin, Louis XIV's wife. Women here are blonde, they have blue eyes, while I am brunette, and my Mediterranean complexion stands out. Even the English language gets me into trouble!"

The Queen started to cry, saying she wanted to know who her rival was. Her soul could not find its peace until she could learn more about her. I comforted the poor miserable soul in front of me as much as I could under the circumstances, asking her to have a little patience to see exactly what the situation was. She did not have any time to waste, though, so she sought out one of her English servants and asked about it, with the latter becoming frightened and kneeling before her. She did, however, confirm the situation to Catarina who felt then that her mother had sold her for a few pennies, only for the sake of their country's security in relationship with Spain. I took her hands and kissed her, and told her that I knew the King was a womanizer and that her situation was inescapable. She had to answer back, to fight back, in silence; she really could do nothing about it, she just had to take it all as it was. She was the unwanted Catholic Queen of England. We had to find some pleasant things to do; we could have not complained our whole life. So I rang the bell, and my two servants came in. The English servant became frightened and knelt down when they saw the Queen. It was my turn then to "cross-examine" her and she told us everything out of fear.

"His Majesty, the King, has had many mistresses, some for a long term, others for a shorter term; he also has many children out of wedlock," my servant went on. "His current favorite is about to give birth to their second child, and she is here in this palace, in Hampton Court Palace."

18

Catarina gave a short cry and took her handkerchief to her mouth. I helped her lie down and I gave her my smelling salts; after that she felt better. She ordered the servant to go; she knew then where Charles had gone after leaving her room. The servant continued as she was ordered:

"Her name is Barbara Villiers. She is married to Roger Palmer, who is an exceptional man. Barbara is quite lovely. She has pale skin and very beautiful eyes, but also a volcanic temperament and indecent conduct. The King does not like women who pray too much, but he adores this kind of women, the loose, rakish kind. Barbara has been involved with the King for two years and married for three."

I thanked her for the information and gestured for them to leave. In the meantime, Marcela, my Portuguese servant, had set the fire and was waiting for Becky to finish what she had to say. After they left, a graveyard silence settled on us. Dawn crept slowly in and a thick fog lingered over the Thames. I told her it was a good thing that she did not have to deal from the very beginning with this relative of the Buckingham dukes. That immoral, unvirtuous woman is two years younger than the Queen. She does not know anything about God, and she was soon to give birth to another bastard.

"But I want to see her, Juliana! My soul is burning unless I see her, then I shall come to terms with my fate, and I shall spend the rest of my life praying next to you. Just imagine that I have to give an heir to England! This is a sad state of affairs!"

I could not talk her into giving up that plan. She wanted to feel pain deep down her soul. She asked me to find out where that woman's apartment was, and then she went to get dressed and ready for breakfast, which is what I did also, continuing to draw information out of Becky, who told me exactly where in the palace Barbara lived.

Right after breakfast, during which the King had been present and acted very kindly, to the barely suppressed disgust of the Queen, Catarina hurried to set her plan into motion. She wanted to go there alone, so she waited until the King left to attend to his own business before she moved to action. She ordered me to remain in her apartment, and she went down the same corridor to a farther apartment. Their meeting was brief. Catarina opened the door without knocking or being announced. She looked in silence at her husband's mistress, who was lying in bed all swollen by the advanced pregnancy. When Barbara understood what was going on, Catarina shouted at her, "I am the Queen!" Barbara cast the Queen a terrible look. Catarina came near the bed, without saying a single word to the woman, who became hysterical and started to shriek. In the Queen's

19

presence, none of the servants could speak. The mistress's cries hit the wall without Catarina making a move. Finally a lady entered the room, to the despair of the favorite, who was supposed to remain hidden, and gently took the Queen by her hand and led her out in silence. The lady told the servants to go away, and when there were only the three of us left, she knelt down and kissed the Queen's hand. Finally, she spoke:

"My name is Anne Hyde, Duchess of York, and wife to the King's brother. I'm glad I was there, by my Queen's side, in that miserable moment! Your Majesty, you need allies, and you do not have them. Unfortunately, Charles is a man who loves pleasures of any kind; you will not change him. You are wrong if you think you will change that attitude of his. My father was the one who negotiated this marriage which makes you suffer from the very first moment. I apologize on his behalf, though he is never going to find out about this meeting of ours. You don't really have much choice. You are Catholic and so am I; maybe you will give birth to a child soon, and you will somehow be safe."

The Queen's face brightened when she learned who the woman in front of her was. She thanked her for her help and hoped that she would be her ally and friend, to which the Duchess agreed gladly; then she left, after she made a lovely bow, to which Catarina responded, smiling. The Queen felt better then, and she knew how bad the mistress must have felt when she, through her silence and steely look, made her scream like an insane person.

"I am the Queen," Catarina said then, standing up and looking out of the window.

CHAPTER 3

Everyone knows that all the walls in a royal court have eyes and ears. The palace we were in was no exception to this rule; thus the King learned soon about the encounter between the two ladies and the fact that Anne, his sister-in-law, took his wife out of Barbara's room. In his own way, Charles was like a child; he wanted it all, and he also wanted peace between the two religions, as well as the freedom to have fun with other women. He was rather short of money, but he managed.

When he encountered his wife, she was withdrawn and quiet in her boudoir. I was away from her at that moment. Catarina stood up and made a curt bow without uttering a word, but it seemed that she had prepared her words in silence, the right words to tell the King. So before he said anything, she spoke:

"Your Majesty, my husband, I've noticed with astonishment that a certain lady shall give birth any moment now to your second child with her. I've seen her and she is beautiful. My charms are not even a quarter of hers. I've realized that you will never love me and that you will never be faithful to a single woman. I am terribly sorry that I cannot change your character for the better; however, you could have been more sensitive, and at least in our first days together, you could have not forced me to live under the same roof with her. I was raised differently. I grew up in a monastery, together with my Lady of Honor, the Countess of Alfambra. The etiquette at my father's court is very strict and quite severe. I've noticed here it is the opposite. I do not deny the fact that all Kings have mistresses; it's just that with a bit of discretion, one can keep up appearances and a certain degree of communication between the two spouses, for their own good and for the nation's good. I grieve simply because there will never be something like this between us. I knew even

21

when I was in Lisbon that you have had many mistresses and many children with them, but I hoped, in my naiveté, that I would be able to change you, even if not by my Mediterranean beauty. I have lost all hope! On my first night here, you left me to go and see your favorite lady, and that hurt me. I am all alone here, I have no ally, nobody is on my side, and everyone hates me because I'm Catholic. I want to go home, I want you to get a divorce as soon as possible! I am suffocating here! I no longer wish to be your wife! I miss the peace in my family, and I prefer my insane brother's outbursts to the situation I am in right now. Find a wife having the same religion as you, and the whole country will be content. For certain no one will stand in your way in accepting the separation from me – I would say quite the contrary!"

That monologue, during which Charles just stood and watched, showed just how good our English teacher was. We had started coming to terms with the language and learning it. But the King did not notice her English. He was dumbfounded. He did not expect such words to come out of his kind and pious wife's mouth.

"Madam, I do not want to divorce! It is true that you are not an ideal beauty, but you do have something that all my mistresses lack: you have a soul, and you have education. It is only natural, since you come from a royal house. I tell you in all sincerity that I cannot restrain myself from the sin of debauchery, but I solemnly swear to you with all my heart that you shall be treated with respect from now on. After the lady in question comes back into society, she shall present her sincere apologies to you for confronting you. It was indeed an error of mine to bring her into the same palace with you. I ask my Queen for forgiveness! You are the Queen of a country where everyone is fighting for everything, but especially for religion. I have continually tried to negotiate peace regarding this topic, but it does not seem to work. Madam, please do not go away! I do not love you, but I do have other feelings for you. I do look up to you, and I shall always support you. You are bound to me in front of God, no matter how many divorces there might be pronounced! And now if you will please excuse me, I shall withdraw!"

They both bowed to each other, and the King left the room. When she saw me later, Catarina was firmly convinced that this was her cross to bear, and she decided to bear it. At least Charles had been honest with her, and everything was now clear between them. She would not be required to attend all the balls and feasts held by the King, except for official ones; she was to be a cloistered Queen, without a grand court, and even if she already had English Ladies of Honor, she preferred me, our native language, and the chapel where we would pray most of the time.

As he left the Queen's room, Charles was struck by her tact and intelligence. She was different from anyone he had met until then; he regretted he could not love her. That was not possible for him. He would do his duty only because he wanted a heir, and that was it. He assumed that she would do her duty as well, if not for England, then at least out of respect for the Catholic family life. When he entered his room, Edward Hyde found him alone and lost in thoughts.

Charles told him everything that had happened and more, namely that Barbara wanted to become a Lady of Honor after she was in grace again and after she recovered from the pregnancy. Hyde answered that that was impossible and that one could not possibly believe Barbara Palmer's excuses would matter to the Queen. Yet the King had to come up with a compromise, both the apologies and the title of Lady of Honor were requested. Hyde just shrugged his shoulders, putting some papers before the King for him to sign, and informed him about many State matters to which the King had to give consent. That very night, the Queen learned about her husband's plans and became furious. She wrung her hands and paced the floor from one end of the room to the other. I could not comfort her; nothing calmed her nerves. She could only sit and wait for that woman to take the first step after she recovered from her delicate condition. The Countess of Castlemaine gave birth the following week to a little boy whom she named after the King. The Queen immediately left the palace and went to the royal official residence in London, to St. James Palace, where she withdrew into her apartment, which she seldom left. During that painful time, the Queen ordered me to look for the husband of that influential woman who, with her whims, practically ran the Kingdom. She learned that ever since he had returned from his journey, Charles left the affairs of state to Edward Hyde and began to party. Shortly after that, the Court's morals began to suffer, imitating those of the King, to the despair of Parliament, which had to keep on approving requests for money, especially for Barbara Villiers Palmer.

Not caring for this way of spending time, Catarina did not take part in those nights of debauchery. She would rather pray, talk to me, or sleep, if noises did not reach her. She was pregnant, and I was the only one who knew that. She was somehow relaxed and happy about this wonderful consolation. The King had not learned it yet. How could she have told him when he was never to be found, as he was taking daily walks between Hampton and St. James and entering the Queen's perimeter only by accident. Of course he found out eventually, and his outraged mistress delivered him some biting reproaches, to which Charles merely shrugged his shoulders.

"My dove, she is the Queen; she has to give me a legitimate successor, and I want to let you know that if you want the position of Lady of Honor to my wife, you must ask her to forgive you for your behavior on your first meeting with her. It is give and take, and you must treat her with great deference and respect, and you will get the title.

"What?" Barbara said, frowning. "What am I to you? Only the one who gets pregnant every year? The one who left her husband and forgot about honor?"

The discussion continued on this same note, only it was obvious that Charles was not impressed by the caprices of his beautiful mistress, who composed herself when she realized she could do nothing to change the situation. They took leave from one other on amicable terms, and the King went to his wife for the next round. The Queen was supposed to give her consent concerning Barbara. But she deferred that for the evening, for Catarina received Hyde as her guest. Palmer was waiting in line at the reception desk, and the King did not want to have to deal with him. Palmer's wife had already made him tired enough.

Catarina listened to Edward Hyde as he told her and warned her about the King's desire regarding his favorite.

"I do not want her near me," she replied, "but I suppose I have no choice. I should not fight this. Let her apologize first, and then we'll talk about it." She no longer listened to Hyde, and he realized that, so he bowed and left the room, respectfully greeting Palmer at the door and then leaving quickly.

When Roger Palmer entered the room, the Queen was standing and responded to his greeting in a very polite manner. One could see that he was a tormented man. Catarina informed him about the birth of the child "that she could not congratulate him on," about Barbara's desire to become her Lady of Honor, and the fact that she could not oppose the King. She also told the count that she was ashamed to confront him about this situation when she had no support from anyone.

Roger Palmer told the Queen that he had made the decision to separate from his wife, but without getting a divorce, because he was Catholic and that seemed to him to be a sin before God, who united them a couple of years before. The Queen appreciated his sacrifice. Even if he made it for someone unworthy, yet it was still a sacrifice. She grew to like the count and told him straightforwardly, "This couple unites us, Count,"

24

and the discussion ended there; afterwards Catarina remained only with me.

Indeed, the poor man separated from his wife, and her affairs depended entirely upon her alone. She had her things sent to her apartment in St. James and thus had cleared her honor. Barbara was not sad at all. She had the King on her side, even though he cheated on her, too, sinning with some other women.

When she made her appearance at the Court, she shone with freshness and beauty. Men's eyes were all on her, but they kept their distance, for she was not theirs; meanwhile, the count of Castlemaine, her legal husband, pretended not to see her. It was an odd situation to chase one's wife away from home, but people did not feel sorry for her. She was arrogant and full of venom against everyone who stood in her way.

She did not feel humiliated when she asked for the Queen's forgiveness for her miserable behavior; she was brash. It was terribly difficult for Catarina to forgive such a viper. She was suffering, and what she wanted most was to leave the ceremony room and go to her small chapel and cry. She knew that after that gesture, she would have to accept her as her Lady of Honor. The King had made only a few allusions, without explicitly saying so, but she understood, for she already knew about it. She caught the eye of Charles's favorite's husband who was leaning against a pillar watching that masquerade from a distance.

The Queen withdrew soon after her gesture of forgiveness, and we went together to her room. She began to cry and not even the baby inside her made her stop. The pain in her heart was coming out through every pore of her being. I told her that maybe this was God's will, maybe this was her cross to bear, and she just replied to me, "Maybe" and nothing more. She confessed to me that her womb hurt and that she would like to lie down, and for me to read something to her. While I was on the third page, she fell asleep. I covered her more warmly, put some more wood on fire, and went to my apartment. What a sad situation and how beautiful she was, that woman, and how quickly she recovered after birth!

My Queen's peace lasted only as long as the night, because the King wanted to see her in the morning. I left them alone. Charles asked of her what she had been waiting to be asked by him; she tried to fight it, sweet thing, but her husband promised her that she would be treated with respect and that she could not fight this situation. Catarina, her eyes in tears, took her hand to the womb, and accepted it, asking the King to leave her alone, for she was not feeling well. Those pains would not go away, so I sent for a doctor. He came and carefully examined Catarina. She was losing blood, and her pregnancy was in danger. Agitation had destroyed her hope of giving birth to a child as well. The King was in Barbara's apartment when he learned the news that he had lost his heir. His mistress laughed noisily.

"Chase her away, darling, she is no good!" she said.

"She will be my wife until death, even if she is not going to have any more babies!" the King said, and then went to see the Queen.

She was sleeping, under the influence of some powders the doctor gave her. The priests were by her side, and so was I. By looking at her husband, I could tell that he was not indifferent to her. He felt she was alone, helpless, rejected, and unhappy. He had some feelings for her, maybe brotherly love or fondness, but not husbandly love. I realized then that we would never leave England because of those strange feelings that the King had. When Catarina opened her eyes, he took her hand in his and kissed it. She tried to shift her look, but Charles slightly moved her head toward him.

"These priests and the Countess of Alfambra are my witnesses that whether you give birth to a heir or not, I will not bear grudges against you. James, my brother, shall reign. It's all the same to me, once I am no longer King. Let them fight over God until they get tired," he went on, smiling. "I shall always have for you a feeling I cannot describe – which does not prevent me, however, from having mistresses. I shall help you at all times, I shall be available for you and I shall put no pressure on you, but there is nohing more I can do for you. I cannot stay and pray all day long, nor can I spend my whole time reading. I do not want to change, and you are my wife, namely the Queen, and you will not return to Portugal, for which you yearn so much. Try to accept this idea and have a court of your own, if mine is too outrageous. Now, I will kindly ask you to excuse me, and accept my plan. We must work together in this. And one more thing, with regard to Barbara, she is not my only paramour, even if she thinks she is the sun in the sky. Her days of glory will come to an end one day. I think I do not betray you so much, because I do not lie to you, but I lie to her!"

That being said, the King left the room, leaving us all astonished and gaping. Thus my suppositions that he felt something for Catarina proved right, only he did not know what. The priests began making the sign of the cross and praying. They did not understand the King's behavior at all, but they advised Catarina to think about what her husband had told her. She needed people around her. She was still young, she could have found pleasant occupations, which were also decent for that matter. I knelt by her bed and kissed her hands.

26

"Dear friend," she told me, "I shall accept my fate and I shall withdraw into my corner, together with you and a few other people. He has been so honest about everything and he has confessed his helplessness. He deserves to be forgiven! He is the husband that God gave me. He is my cross to bear. And then, imagine how this woman will feel when she finds herself abandoned with her children. She is beautiful, but rather silly. I shall live to see her fall."

Catarina was too good for the place where she ended up, so she swallowed the bitter cup of despair. She had been through hell, and all she could do was to rise up. After she spent a few days in bed, she rose and said she felt better, but her beautiful smile was gone. She had started receiving people who paid visits to her. The Duchess of York was the first to kiss her and wish her quick recovery. Then came the Catholic noblemen, among whom was the favorite's husband, and in the end a few Protestants. The King waited for one more month before he officially introduced Barbara, Countess of Castlemaine, as the Queen's Lady of Honor.

There were rumors at the ceremony that she was pregnant again by the King, but Catarina had closed her wings, hiding her heart that was starting to heal. She received the countess with coldness, yet politely; they had tried having a conversation, but the effort was futile. That beautiful woman was just a toy; one could not have found a serious topic to discuss with her. When the talk ended, the Queen withdrew to her apartment with me. Barbara frowned because the door was closed, and the Queen gave in only upon the King's insistence. Catarina looked around at the faces of James, Anne and her father, of other Catholics, of her husband whom she noticed was disgusted, and left, her head held high. The King loved her, she was sure of it.

We went through a door and entered the Queen's personal chapel, and we started praying out loud. When we finished, the Queen's forehead was relaxed; peace had settled upon her. She hugged me and smiled the way I had seen only back at the monastery. She had made the decision to relax, to have fun, and to do what she pleased. She learned to play cards, she held fancy balls and tea soirées. Tea was something new to the English people, and the Queen required a certain protocol for these intimate meetings. Her court was a small one, made up especially of Catholics, to the despair of the Protestant noblemen who hated her and complained to the King, who was not at all interested in these complaints. He always had the same retort: "Respect the Queen and treat her properly. She has my permission to do whatever she pleases. I do stand by her side!" All his life, the King was dualistic, siding with neither the Anglican nor the Catholic Church. On every issue, he would just wind them around his little finger, to the despair of the noblemen and Parliament.

And yet the Queen did have a moment of major sadness in her withdrawal. She had received a letter telling her that her mother had been removed from the governance of the Kingdom, and the mad Alfonso was running it together with his friend, the Count of Castelo Melhor. What was worse was that Luiza de Guzman had been sent to the monastery. She pictured her mother sad and helpless, walking to and fro at the monastery. With Luiza's agility and bright mind, Catarina wondered how she would fill her time while being confined there. She realized that her mother could not possibly read prayers continuously and she was thinking that she herself, the Queen of England, was much more free, even if she was not loved. Alfonso on the throne shocked her more, though. What was he doing with his nervous outbursts? Was Portugal going to fall to pieces? The Spanish were smelling something, for certain. She loved her country and her people, but there was nothing she could do for them. She was far away, and she could not leave England. The letter also said that the King was paralysed on one side, and that since he was sitting down most of the time, he had put on much weight. The one who really ran things was that friend of his, the Count Castelo Melhor, because Pedro, the Duke of Beja, was still very young.

I shared her pain, thinking more about her brother Pedro, who was in his early years in life. She gave me the letter to keep; she was afraid it might be seen by someone and taken away. There were so many ladies around her who were claiming their rights for the Queen's company.

This is how autumn passed and winter settled in, with the wonderful feast and the joy of the Lord's Birth. We were supposed to attend the masked ball held by the King between Christmas and New Year's Eve. It was an official ball, so we had started to get ready for it. Barbara Villiers had again begun to put on weight. Her pregnancy was visible, but she displayed it all very happily everywhere she went. She had announced she would take part in this festivity, taking all necessary precautions. By then, the Queen was used to the King's favorite's pregnancies. She was counting them on her fingers: this was Barbara's third pregnancy. And then she smiled, thinking of what her husband had told her when she had the miscarriage. Barbara's star was going to go down sooner or later.

CHAPTER 4

What a ball, the madness and the debauchery! The Queen and I had decided to mask so that everyone could recognize us. There was no point in hiding under masks one more complicated than the other. We wanted to stay as far as possible from the crowd. The King had a costume, too, but his height betrayed him. The others pretended they didn't know who he was, and treated him like a stranger. While one wore a mask, almost everything was allowed. Our shock was that Barbara did indeed show up. We had hoped she would not put in an appearance in her condition. We knew that her husband was also among the guests, but we did not strive to look for him and recognize him. The Countess of Castlemaine was dressed up like a Catholic nun, to everyone's complete shock. She had gone beyond any limit of decorum. In such a costume, her belly could stay loose without the corset. She was a nun with a Queen's crown on her head, as an allusion to the fact that she was really in charge. The King's first reaction was astonishment; then he started laughing out loud, thus irritating the noblemen present at that celebration. The latter, no longer in the mood for the ball, had started forming groups or getting near the Queen, visibly anxious for a decent hour to come, so that they could leave.

Charles approached his mistress, and they started dancing next to the other pairs keen on moving. Catarina remained still, hardly controlling her nerves and tears. Royal etiquette did not allow her to leave, not yet. That was the moment when Palmer sat next to us, revealing himself and showing us a red, sweaty forehead.

"There is nothing I can do to comfort you, Count," Catarina said in a low voice. "This is a woman I can neither understand nor classify in one way or another, but the costume is outrageous, worse than any in the crowd. I know you wish you had withdrawn. I want the same thing, but we will do that in two hours. We cannot help it!"

"I am not asking for any consolation, my Queen. I ask only for permission to stay next to Your Majesty. This is a more isolated place where I can be quiet. I shall leave in two hours. I am a cuckold, even if I have been separated from her for some time now. I shall go home, and tomorrow I'm going to the countryside. I shall go hunting, I shall try the simple and small things in life, and New Year's Eve will find me all alone, praying to God to give me strength. My parents warned me about her a few years ago, but I was enslaved by her beauty, which increases or decreases depending on these pregnancies coming every year. And yet I forgive her and I pity her. The King has also other mistresses besides her. I am surprised that she can put up with this, and also at the way she clings onto the sovereign! She is like an castaway in the middle of the sea who keeps on hanging onto a board, then loses her grip on it, and so on and so forth."

"I can see very well that you loved her. You are more miserable and unhappy than I am." Catarina held out her hand to him, who pressed it lightly, then took it to his lips. "Who is that domino, Juliana? The King bowed to her, to the nun's despair. Everything is like a show; I almost feel like laughing, if I could forget my own unhappiness."

Indeed, the King rushed to bow to Barbara, then took the domino to dance. I immediately recognized her; it was "La Bella Stuart," a beauty of a woman, a distant relative of the King, apparently born in Paris. She was no older than sixteen, and she was fresh like a rose bud. She was not married and much younger than the King's official mistress.

When that withdrawal hour came, to everyone's joy, we took leave of Roger Palmer and made our way to the King, to ask his permission to leave. Gallantly he granted it, kissing the Queen's hand and bowing before her. The Count of Castlemaine left as well, and right after him, many of the Catholic noblemen did the same. Palmer had no authority over his wife, for they were officially separated.

The King's court glittered at that Christmas ball, but not from the richness displayed or the carefully chosen menu or the rooms' splendid decorations, but through the debauchery that the people of the Court were lending themselves to, under those masks. Pair after pair, they withdrew toward the windows, hidden behind the draperies. Others would curse each other while smiling and pretending to have pleasant conversations. It was obvious that they were of different confessions, and recognizing each other, they did not miss the chance to have a tilt at each other. All this before the eyes of an distracted King who cared only about the domino next to him.

Out of the Catholic noblemen, there were left only Edward Hyde, his daughter Anne, and the King's brother, the Duke of York. In between the two spouses was the man who truly ruled England, and the old man spoke in a low, sad voice about the King's ingratitude.

"The King," he said, "forgot about his father's death; he forgot about his brothers' deaths and about Cromwell's disinterment and burial under the scaffold at Whitehall, actually the burial of the remains left after the madding crowd had walked his corpse through London. Unfortunately, the King is interested only in his mistresses, whom he betrays off-handedly. Look at that domino! Rumor has it that she has not given in to the King, thanks to the Countess of Castlemaine. The Queen had a miscarriage because of this, but the countess is wringing her hands, being ignored, and carrying the King's baby in her womb. Not to mention the Count! He is the official cuckold of the Court. Orgy is everywhere now that theaters have re-opened and outrage us with their productions. What kind of banquet is this, without the Queen? He did not grant a single dance to her, poor woman. I think, James, that you will rule England, even if you are Catholic. You will see that you will! The Queen shall not give him a heir, and he couldn't care less. He's amused by a more contentious fight between the two religions. And now this craze of a code bearing my name, which I do not acknowledge since I am a Catholic, the "Clarendon Code." Everything for the consolidation of the Anglican Church positions. Just listen to that; they want to approve that all these Protestants say the same prayers, that is, have the same requests for God!"

Let's let the Lord mull over that question in the company of the two spouses approving him; let's also let the Count of Castlemaine go to sleep in a well warmed room in his house, and let's follow the Queen, who left from that horrible ball with me. Once we arrived in the Queen's apartment, she took off her jewels, so as to feel more comfortable. Marisa helped Catarina to get undressed, and being obviously more relaxed, Catarina sat in an armchair, after the servant left.

"Have you noticed, Juliana," she said calmly, "how these people hate me for my religion? It is as if I were an intruder, and not their mistress. I wonder what those books of theirs teach them. To hate everybody who is of a different confession? What joy they felt when I asked permission to withdraw, and the King granted it immediately! Sometimes Charles seems rational and I see a certain kindness in his eyes, but most of the time he is looking only for joy and pleasure in life, and he

31

is so selfish and makes everyone suffer. And you know what, Juliana? Sometimes I think he does not even realize it. I think he is still a spoiled little boy who asks for a toy, only to throw it away afterwards. I think his favorite toys are women who fall for him. He dismisses them, he receives them, just like a child who searches through his toy box for a toy that is at the bottom of the case. And I don't like how he dresses up and smartens up. He's like a woman sometimes."

Then she sighed, tired of too much talk. To change the topic, I started reminding her about our happy childhood, about the Christmas holidays spent in Portugal where the weather was warm, about presents, our parents, forgiveness, and Jesus's birth. I saw that all of that made her happy, living through the memories of the joy back then. For a single moment, she remembered her mother confined at the monastery by her brother. She stood up and went to the window. It was cold, even if the fire was burning pleasantly in the fireplace.

"Look, Juliana, it's snowing! I don't know if I have ever seen snow before."

I also stood up and stood with her by the window. It was just a snow shower. I liked it, too, though I did not open the window. The Queen thought of Roger Palmer then and pulled me toward the bed where we sat down.

"Poor man! Do you remember how much he insisted that these two children be given his name and thus acknowledged by him? He insisted that they were his children. How he baptized little Charles in the Catholic religion, and Barbara was outraged and re-baptized him Anglican? And the King, only to pour salt on the wound, acknowledged them both? I so pity him, but he did what he had to do in the long run; he chased that woman away from his home."

"My dear Catarina, that did not wipe the spots off his honor. You've seen how people laugh at him and think of him as the official cuckold of the Court," I said.

"He holds his head high with pride," the Queen added. "He took the blow right in the breech, but he shows himself in society, he minds his business, so naturally you would be inclined to believe it is real. I for one believe, though, that he and his family suffer a lot, and that they all make considerable efforts to keep up the appearance of normalcy. Shameful woman, she's had such a well-mannered man, and she just trod on him! They say that the Count of Chesterfield had something to say about their first child. Fortunately for her, Charles acknowledges it all, and he is the ultimate father of all his mistress's children. Sometimes, I feel like

32

smiling, but it iss a shame and it is late. We must go to bed. Everything is quiet now, I suppose."

The Queen kissed and embraced me, allowing me to go to my room. When I lay down in bed, I tried to recall that unforgettable night, but the thread broke and sleep took me in its arms until morning. I woke up rather late, but still at a decent hour for a morning after a half-slept night. I got dressed and left myself in the hands of the maid for hair styling and the rest of the details regarding my outfit. I wanted to go to Catarina as soon as I was ready. I found her getting dressed.

"Juliana, listen to what they're telling me," she said hastily.

The servants had told the Queen all the rumors, which we knew about, with regard to that outrageous party. Laura had told our sovereign how Barbara had made a fool of herself in front of everybody, how everybody was laughing at her behind her back, gossiping while covering their mouths with their hands. Charles had left her sitting on a chair after a dance and paid attention only to that lovely domino. Everybody noticed how the King's favorite lady hardly concealed her tears, wringing and twisting her hands, but that was not all, Laura said. The King left together with that domino, without speaking or making any gesture toward the one who gave him their third child. After Charles left, a prolonged "oh" could be heard everywhere, as well as snickering. The favorite spent some more time there, but not too much, and then left, holding her head high, proud like a stork, under the others' amused looks. The party and the gossip went on even after she left, only more noisily, since there wasn't anyone to record that. Lord Clarendon and the Duke of York had been gone for some time, so that the palace was full of the party guests who were wondering whom to feel more sorry for, the Queen or the mistress. Most of the drunkards' voices were shouting sympathy for the mistress, for the Queen had her prayers, since she was a Catholic.

"I think we're blessed we have our prayers, my dear Queen," I said, quickly. Catarina responded immediately that I was right.

We had taken our breakfast in the Queen's rooms, to the irritation of the other English Ladies of Honor, who were only too seldom granted access to the sovereign's rooms. They were dissatisfied, but had no one to whom they could complain about it, for the King was always caught up with something, and even when the topic was brought up, it was quickly closed by the fact that Charles was loyal to his wife and demanded maximum respect for the Queen and her desires. The Ladies of Honor could do nothing but acquiesce and smile to the Catholic Queen, full of prayers, which they did not attend since they were Anglican.

33

People found out who that domino was: she was Frances Stuart, a distant relative of the King's, one of ravishing beauty, who was no older than sixteen. She was born in Paris, and after the Restoration, she came back to her parents' country. She was not married, and rumor had it that she had not given in to the King, who was quite taken with her. Frances knew about Barbara Villiers and her entire story, and they said that was the very reason she would never give in to the King, who was head over heels in love with her and was waiting for the beautiful young lady to finally give in to his perseverance. Someone followed them, and indeed, the King was left outside at the door of his relative, not entering her room. He appeared upset, making for Barbara's room, his consolation always. What else could she have done except let him in and swallow all her anger?

One can learn so many things, most of them evil, in such a vast Court as the Court of England. One becomes impolite, a liar, a traitor, in love in the evening and forgetful in the morning, without any of those involved being angry about it. We began to get used to these things and look around us, while keeping our distance. Everything was like a gilded show at the Court of King Charles II of England. We, but especially the Queen, had more of a secondary and decorative role, rather unpleasant for the Court, because of our simple, modest, and strict conduct. Barbara won that day, too, at least that was what she wanted to think, but the Queen had started to know her husband well; the star of his favorite lady would soon go down, and "la Bella Stuart" was not necessarily going to replace her. There were also so many other available women; one could not even keep track of them, but we were not interested in counting the King's mistresses.

CHAPTER 5

And so the winter passed by and the cold seemed to have lessened; London changed its look. The trees were green, they bloomed, then lost their blooms; parks invited walks on sunny days. Once spring settled in, something else appeared besides the beauty of the vegetation: the ugliness of the side streets, where mud ran knee-deep unless one had some wonderful means of riding by carelessly, splashing everyone on their way to the recently opened theaters, which at that time had brought woman to the fore, to the despair of the prim and straitlaced wives of the noblemen. London had also exposed the vagabonds, the pickpockets, and other such groups, who would wait for the ladies to come out of the theater to relieve them of their jewels and the gentlemen, of their thick coins purses. We were not interested in that, nor was the King. He had three major concerns, all interconnected. The first issue was Barbara, who had become more and more jittery because of her pregnancy; Miss Frances Stuart, who would not give in to the King, which drove him mad; and the Queen, who was seriously ill. Catarina had been unconscious for some time, and when she spoke, she would simply start raving. Doctors were astonished and did not have medical resources to heal the Queen. I was the only one who sat by her side. When she would shout and cry, she insisted that she had given birth to a child, and the King would finally approve her.

During that period, I noticed that the King seemed to have feelings I could not possibly identify. It was not love, since he had stated in no uncertain terms that should the Queen pass away, he would propose to Frances. Still, there was a certain fondness, affection, fellowship, a strong alliance between him and Catarina. He came frequently to see how his wife was, even if afterwards he would go to see his mistresses or have fun at the theater or some party full of young ladies handed to him on a plate by their families.

35

I just felt that the King had something good inside his soul. Then I thought that the suffering during his youth had most surely had an impact on him, and it was as if he had been trying to make up for those old times. But I was grateful to him for the look cast on my friend when he sat on the bed next to her, gently, so as not to wake her. I pitied him, just as I pitied his favorite lady, who was supposed to give birth any day then, and who out of ambition had to put up with Frances, who would not give in to the King.

Fever took hold of Catarina, and wet cloths dried quickly on her forehead. The doctors said that her brain was boiling and that she would not live much longer, for she had no chance of recovering. I was distraught. I thought that I would have to leave England while she remained there in London. I could not enjoy seeing my sunny Portugal again without Catarina. I was tired and I wanted all of this to be over somehow. The King, seeing me every day so attached to his Queen, had his eyes set on me as his new victim. I was afraid, but I prayed to God for that King to have mercy on that sick woman.

One morning while I was looking for something to do near Catarina's bed, the King suddenly came in, seemingly amazed that I had no support, no help, as if he really had something on his mind. Then he came near me and took my hand. I shivered and started praying at the same time when a clear and familiar voice saved me:

"Leave her, my King. She belongs to me; you have so many ladies you can conquer...."

It was the Queen, who spoke coherently after a long time. The King let me go and ran out, calling the doctors, who took note of the miracle. The Queen had recovered and the fever was gone. Catarina continued to look at Charles, as if waiting for an answer that he gave her:

"The countess is all yours. I'm so glad you feel better. I'm going to tell everyone this news!"

Upon saying that, the King cheerfully left the room in his own peculiar way. He took the news to Barbara, who had given birth and was staying in bed. This child was also a boy, baptized Henry. The favorite was happy for the Queen, she teased the King, laughing at his making plans with young Frances Stuart. The news spread throughout the Court, some being happy while others were not, according to each one's heart.

I thanked Catarina for having been the angel that saved me; I held her hands and cried out of joy that she had recovered. I was truly happy. I knew that the King would keep his promise, and I also knew that the Queen would soon feel better. Indeed, that night she let me sleep in my

36

own apartment; she had tied a bell to a string which ran from her room to mine so that she could call me anytime. I really needed some rest, so after having slept in the armchair in her room, my own bed seemed like heaven on earth to me, even if I was in a hostile country.

Catarina was feeling better every single day, under my care and that of her two faithful servants. Life had prevailed. When she first sat in the armchair, we celebrated with tea and we lifted many prayers to God, along with our good priests. It had been an intimate reunion with only Portuguese there. Little by little, we both got color back in our cheeks and we started going out in the palace gardens. Then, we had to endure the presence of all the Ladies of Honor and their rude remarks, but sickness had taught us well. The Queen would always say that she had woken up from the other land. She had decided to treasure life, without depending on the King or another nobleman.

Also in this blissful period, to everyone's amazement, Barbara Villiers converted to catholicism. Nobody knew why she did this. Was it because she wanted to be in the graces of a King who wished for religious tolerance or for her husband who was Catholic, and from whom she was separated? Anyway, what is certain is that she did convert. She was, of course, remarkably beautiful, but much more reserved in her relationship with the Queen. She had never again dared offending her to her face. Sometimes I would catch a sarcastic smile on her face when the Queen wasn't watching. She was still sure of her influence over the King. The Catholics had always looked at her with skepticism as far as her new religion was concerned, and her husband's family was quite outraged. Who cared? Obviously, she didn't, nor the Count of Castlemaine, but some whispered that the King would stop by her, to ease his anger. Frances would not give in to him for anything; she did not want to be his mistress; she could have been the Queen. She was an independent girl, very stubborn, young and very beautiful, but reasonable after all. She was only sixteen and she had her whole life ahead of her. Because of her refusals, Barbara had one more pregnancy, then a birth, which outraged the Catholic priests and those faithful to that religion. She gave birth to a girl whom she named Charlotte, whose acknowledged father was the King. Catarina did not react in any way; she had found tranquility regarding her inability to have a child in the balm of her prayers. A Catholic King would succeed to the throne, which did not seem such a bad idea to her. In her own chapel, she had come to accept Barbara, who was giving birth to a child almost every year, and year after year she would become beautiful again, as she was before the pregnancy. The Queen was 26, while the mistress was only 23.

Catarina loved walking in the countryside. We would jump into a carriage, sometimes dressed in simple clothes, and we would enjoy the simplicity of life. We would sit in the shadow of a tree or on the bank of a stream and eat whatever the servants accompanying us had put in the baskets. The King had no idea about our escapades at first, but when he learned about them, he had nothing against them. His wife had to do something to feel good too. The Court was divided: some people held the opinion that it was not appropriate for the Queen to leave as she wished, while others agreed with her, but there were fewer of the latter. Others gave advice to the King, but he did not listen to them, continuing to demand that they respect his wife. He was considered a curiosity to the noblemen. He had so many mistresses besides the official one, and yet he became angry when the Queen was not granted the full respect she deserved. As for us, we liked the ordinary people who knew nothing about the malice at the Court. The Queen's eyes shone, and her forehead would become relaxed. She forgot for awhile about her miserable life. I think she loved the King, but I don't know in what nuance. I was no longer living for myself; I did not have much news about Gaspar, Catarina's cousin, but I had dreams and nights of delight. Night was like a fairytale.

During our outings, when I dared to bring him into discussion, the Queen would laugh at my heart's naivety and purity. I hid nothing from her; I was like an open book to her. She liked listening to me, as I was carefully listening to her as well. We got along so well, to the spite of the other ladies who did not care about their mistress.

And so the year passed by, between quiet and peaceful walks and bitter receptions, kind looks and flashes of obvious hatred. Barbara gave birth to one more baby, that time a boy, making us wonder when she would ever stop. That was her fifth child whom the King acknowledged. Still, it was obvious that their relationship was slowly deteriorating, and that the King would tacitly consider other ladies. The Countess was still his favorite, but she was now tolerating the sovereign's love affairs, which made us believe she had gotten tired, too. I think also that she was tired of so many pregnancies and so many babies around her. Rumor had it that she was seeing other men, too, but I did not try to learn more about that situation; I just let time reveal it all in due season.

Those love affairs moved to the background once the second Dutch war started in 1665. It was then that I lived through a war for the first time in my life, even if not directly with a gun in my hand. At first we were glad for the battles we had won, and then, when the Dutch reached the Thames, we went through indescribable fears. During that period, the hatred was aimed mainly at the Dutch, and my Queen was left in peace. In fact, she wasn't even interested in the Dutch expansion to North Africa and North America. That war started upon the suggestion of Lord Clarendon, and it would end badly for this statesman as well. That good man was assiduously attacked by his enemies, for he was a Catholic, and he was running the country upon Charles's order.

During that war, around early autumn, the plague broke out in London. The Court had to move to Salisbury and let people who remained in London handle it as best they could. It was said that mice had spread the plague as they came in with grain unloaded from ships. It was an ugly period in Charles's reign. People often died in the streets; others were forced to stay at home, being sick, and were given food through the window. Graveyards were full, and the grave diggers had to work continuously until they themselves succumbed to the disease. Toward the end of the contagion, people were simply buried in a common grave. Nobody accompanied them on their last trip, because their relatives were also dead or waiting for their ending. I had the sad fortune to see people suffering from that affliction: they were hideous and desperate with those huge boils. I shall never forget one instance. It happened on the day we were leaving London; a man struck by the plague had stretched his hand toward our carriage, but had not received a penny; instead, what he got was a lash on his back to make him keep his distance. I shall never, ever forget that look on his face, that desperate look begging for a piece of bread. It was a young man, rather pleasant-looking if one disregarded his ragged clothes and the swellings that could be seen through his open shirt. I think that he had become poor because of his disease, for he did not look like a beggar by trade, but rather like a man who had won his bread through honest work. Our carriage passed by quickly, and, through the back window, I could see enough that I would never forget that scene. Only a few survived then.

Catarina's second pregnancy, which she had unfortunately miscarried in 1666, was linked to that plague, or better said, to our stay in Salisbury. Yet, the sorrow was not so great, and we overcame it more easily that time. The King was not angry at all, and Barbara was not pregnant again, probably a sign of the growing distance between them. I knew they were still together, but the flame of love would be quenched from time to time.

Also during that time, the Queen, to the despair of Protestants, ordered that a religious house be built next to St. James Palace, where everybody who wanted to pray for the victims of the plague could come. She had Franciscan monks come from Portugal, and they helped as much as they could. Thus, there was formed a kind of Catholic brotherhood,

39

much to the despair of the English people who were weary of the plague that was then subsiding, weary of the Dutch, and weary of Catholicism; nothing could have been worse to them.

In 1666, as I said before, Catarina had another miscarriage, probably also because of the obvious hatred that people displayed under the pretence of respect. She had withdrawn even more from the life of the Court, in part because everything was turned upside down, given the situation in London.

Most of the houses in the city were built of wood and were really close to one another. Therefore it was not difficult, one year after the plague broke out, for fire to heal the city. Many of those who had survived the plague died of smoke and flame. Thousands of people lost their homes and were wandering lost, looking for a bit of food. Plague, fire, and hunger had brought the capital to its knees, to the despair of the King and his brother. The city burned like a straw fire, including many of the churches at that time. Naturally, scapegoats were found: the Catholics, starting with Lord Clarendon, headed the list. He was accused of bad management of the country, of arranging the King's marriage to an infertile Catholic woman, of the plague, of starting the war against the Dutch, and for the great fire that had destroyed everything. And yet he was not blamed because the King had stopped making children with his mistresses. Not that. And further, he was not blamed because the King had entrusted him with full power, so that he himself could have free reign. The Parliament thus accused good Edward Hyde of high treason, and he had to flee to France. Those days were awful for the Queen and her sister-in-law. Catarina was losing a good adviser, and Anne was losing her father. She knew that she would never see him again, for exile meant "farewell." Thus, the man who had governed England's affairs had to escape to France where he was very well received, but he kept his distance, living privately in Rouen. He did not return to England alive.

Thus, having a carefree playboy King, the Protestants were having much fun at the expense of the Catholics whom they had been oppressing more and more since 1664 through the very Clarendon Code. The Catholics' situation was desperate. They were not allowed to gather in groups; their priests were confined to only a five-mile radius around their parish in which to do their work. That was a restriction of all rights, and yet the Queen had managed to have her religious house built, and anyone who wanted to visit was allowed to do so.

But the Londoners struck again. They had no houses, they had no more tears to shed over their dead, they were dog-poor, while the Queen was taking care of her Catholics near St. James Palace, and the King was indifferent to the advice of people around him, demanding respect for his wife. The English calm had long been destroyed when the Dutch fleet freely advanced on the Thames and burned all our docked ships except for the admiral ship bearing the name of the King. They had taken that back home as a trophy. That was the end of the war, sealed by the peace treaty in Breda; once again, the King accused Edward Hyde for that failure, to Anne's sorrow.

Besides all this, the Queen and I had to pray also for the soul of her mother who had passed away out of anger in the monastery. The pain was tremendous. She had died all alone, without anyone from the family near her. Right after that, the lunatic and paralysed King of Portugal had the impudence to marry Maria Francisca of Savoia. The mourning had not been observed in any way. We were mourning her death, we, the miserable beings, in a boat too small for the troubled ocean we were living in. Of course, the marriage was not consummated. How could it have been? So, without even knowing her, we were deeply commiserating Alfonso's wife. There was nothing that could have been done about that, for Pedro was still under the age when he could have intervened. Europe was watching that situation inside the Braganza House dumbfounded, waiting for Pedro to enter his rights, for he was ten years younger than Catarina. He was just a baby when we left; I could barely remember him. Who knew whether we would ever see him again.

That period was a nightmare, especially living in Salisbury. Barbara was fighting frequently for Charles, who had enormous burdens then, which he would forget in the arms of someone willing to comfort him. Frances Stuart, to the sovereign's complete bewilderment, married Charles Stuart, Duke of Richmond and Lennox, becoming his third wife. But the King ousted the Duke from the Court, appointing him Ambassador to Denmark, and thus coming closer to Frances, to Barbara's despair. She had come to realize that her star was going down, and she was looking for consolation in the arms of other men. Frances's triumph came when her image was minted on a commemorative Britannia medal in memory of the war against the Dutch. That medal retained the lady's beauty in memory for posterity.

When we came back to London, reconstruction was at its height. I think it was late 1667 when we returned. We withdrew to our apartments as soon as we arrived, and everything had been arranged. We didn't go out anymore; we weren't interested anymore in Parliament, or who had taken over the power following Lord Clarendon. We knew there were a few people who weren't exactly getting on well with each other, and that their

41

leader was Lord Arlington. Anne, the Duchess of York's grief hurt us deeply, but there was nothing we could do about it. Women like Catarina and me had no credibility. We were merely decorative, and even that was very rare, on special occasions, and to show that women have an abysmal fate, I can only describe what happened to the beautiful Duchess of Richmond, the young and lovely Frances, the next year.

Destiny made her contract a severe case of smallpox, which left her maimed. Fortunately, her beautiful face remained on that medal. All her plans ceased to exist, and she withdrew to one of her rich domains, never again going out in society. She found a passion in caring for her pets and in playing cards; her career was virtually finished, and she comforted herself alone, for her husband was still in Denmark. After that sad event, we didn't hear much about her; she wasn't really receiving anyone anymore, and the King probably thought he had been fortunate for not having married poor Frances. What would have he done with a woman whose face was simply destroyed?

The King had no time to ask himself that question because unfortunately Catarina, having had two more miscarriages, still left him with no heir, thus having to account for that before Parliament. That legislative forum wanted the sovereign to divorce Catarina and marry a Protestant lady who could have children. The King refused to get a divorce, and thus the conflict between the Anglicans and the Catholics spread. Nobody understood how the King could be so tolerant of that Catholic and infertile woman. Charles repeatedly demanded – God knew for how many times – respect for his Queen, to whom he was faithful, and to whom, even if he was physically unfaithful, he was morally faithful, so to speak. The country had already gotten a heir to the throne, the King said, and that was James, Duke of York, a Catholic, a proper heir. Of course, the Duke realized that if after those love affairs he was still alive, he would reign in a country where his religion was hated by the Anglican one.

Catarina had become a permanent target for the Court. She was grateful to the King for his defense of her, for forgiving her for her helplessness, and for the fact that in a spiritual way, he was faithful to her. Everybody hated her openly; nobody paid respect to her anymore, so that all we had left was prayer, whereby we asked for strength to survive every single day. We never left our apartments anymore except to go to that religious house. Catarina remained faithful to her husband, whom she respected for defending her. We had meals only among ourselves, and sometimes the King would pay us a visit. On those occasions, he would just stare at the Queen without uttering a single word. They would talk a little, mostly with their eyes. I would say that he had appeased his mistresses. Obviously, he would pay visits to Barbara, but not only her, and so she would keep her figure and face still untainted.

The King was bored by that continual antagonism between the two religions. He was even hot-tempered because his peace was troubled by those futile confrontations, as he thought of them. He wanted the Anglicans to be more tolerant of the English of a different confession, so he made one more move, which incited the Protestants to a boiling furor: he came back to his Barbara, to whom he gave Phoenix Park in Dublin. He appointed her Baroness of Nonsuch and Duchess of Cleveland – not to mention that his mistress had been a Catholic for some years by then.

Thus the Court was divided between those saying that the lady was once again in the King's favor, and those who thought those gifts were a kind of a parting gift, with the latter having had enough of the unfortunate influence of the new duchess over the King's life. And they were right. The Duchess of Cleveland had no influence anymore, slowly declining from her role of favorite lady. The Queen felt sorry for her and even had the courage to pay her a visit and tell her to her face. The Duchess did not respond; on the contrary, she was aware that she had acted wrongly toward the Queen, and that maybe she would have had something to gain if she had been Catarina's ally, and not hostile to her. That did not mean they had become friends, but only that the guard had been let down, and that hatred of Barbara had turned into a mixture of indifference and cordiality.

CHAPTER 6

Charles, in his stubborn refusal to get a divorce, and overtly stating his position before Parliament, had created for himself a great deal of financial difficulty. His income had dropped, since he had a wife and a heir, both Catholics. No one wanted to support those people and their consorts. But the King managed as always, thanks to his natural, native talent for survival, which he had proven more than once in his youth. Without making any effort, he ensured himself a substantial annuity for the rest of his life from his cousin across the Channel. Louis XIV, after he lost the decentralization war, assumed the obligation to give money to his cousin every year. The King of France did not ask for anything except Charles's conversion to Catholicism, which the Englishman did not deny; he himself wanted to convert, but unfortunately, he could not set an exact date for that, given the tense religious situation in England. Louis was so strongly in support of Charles's conversion that he wrote to Charles offering to send him a small army of a couple of thousand soldiers to ensure a peaceful religious service for the King's confirmation in Catholicism. With a great deal of tact, the English King pacified his cousin, saying that he would let him know when the service would occur, explaining that those troops would only cause more rumors among the Protestant majority. In London, hatred was more lively than ever, and he needed peace. It seemed that Louis had calmed down and relaxed his zeal, and Charles got the money with nothing required in return. It seemed that he did need money, for in the meantime, two more babies were born from his relationship with another famous mistress at that time.

Those children, too, were acknowledged by their father. The favorite, still in the King's graces, though barely, was comforting herself in the arms of other men, giving birth to her last child in 1672, but that child was never acknowledged by his father.

That year of 1672 was a full one, from the political point of view. The King had started the third Dutch war, to the despair of the English people, who had had enough of so much fighting. That war would soon prove unpopular with the English Parliament, which refused to provide any more money for its continuation. The legislative forum was dissatisfied with the appearance at the King's Court of a new favorite lady, a beautiful young French woman, emerged from nowhere and looking fresh like a fairy. It seems that she had been a French spy at the Court of England. Many had tried to talk to the King about her in that sense, but he heard and saw nothing. Louise de Kerouaille, for that was the lady we are talking about, could squeeze the treasury without actually receiving money because of the extravagant gifts Charles bought for her, from jewels to palaces and other outrageously expensive things. The people made a comparison between Barbara Palmer and her, and everybody agreed that the gifts offered to the English lady had been huge indeed, but they were offered over a longer period, while the spy worked much faster. Barbara Palmer had remained Lady of Honor, but she was only a decorative element.

Along came Louise, who became almost overnight the Queen's *dame de compagnie* and the King's personal advisor, and she hurried to give him a child whom he immediately acknowledged. The Queen no longer reacted to those births, which had multiplied; she had long given up hope of having a baby, and actually Charles no longer paid her visits toward that goal.

We were also inclined to believe that that beautiful Louise was indeed a spy. She was well-mannered, stylish, and moreover, she was extremely respectful to the Queen. Catarina grew to like Louise, and she would rather spend time in her company than in the company of other Ladies of Honor, who were driven mad by that attitude of the Queen, but especially by seeing another Catholic besides the Queen. "The court is full of Catholics!" they shouted, "and everything is happening because of these people." Louise seemed to have been trained for such situations; she would just pass by them, smiling, courteously greeting them, while the Protestant ladies would just grunt, but had to greet her back.

Sometimes I smiled watching those occasions from the shadows. I had never yearned for anything like that. I was considered to be one with the Queen, which made me almost invisible. The relationship between us two and the favorite lady made the King happy. He said that at last, "the ladies get on well with each other," moving on to see the other neglected Ladies of Honor. Louise could enter the Queen's rooms almost any time,

45

even if, pretending to court and flatter me, she would knock on my door first; then I would inform the Queen about it, and she would see her, thus outraging the Court. She did not react either when the King had an affair with a courtesan, and its consequence, namely a baby, started to show.

"Yes," Catarina told me one day, "she is a spy, Juliana! She shows no expression of emotion on her angelic face. Do you remember Barbara? She would react differently. She would tear down the palace with her screaming, and now, it's as if she no longer exists. Do you remember Portugal, my sweet Juliana? You followed me in this bane, and you suffer next to me, but I never imagined life like this! So much hatred!"

I kissed her hands and told her that I suffered only because she suffered. What could I have done in Portugal? I would have gotten married; I would have been immersed in family life to my fullest, too quiet in that sunny country. The Queen smiled at me and hugged me, then took my hand and we went to her room, where we sat down, she at her writing table, and I in front of her.

"I have news from Portugal, my dear friend! Here is the letter. It came intact, as they all do," the Queen told me, handing me the letter like a trophy.

Letters often reached us with difficulty, and only through the Franciscan brothers, who had their ways and channels, unknown to the world. I confess that I was anxious as always when we received letters from our country. The sender was, of course, the Duke of Beja, the Regent. He told us about the exiled King, who was growing more and more intransigent and cloudy in his thinking, about the difficulty of people around him to take care of him. He reminded us of his little girl who was three back then in 1672, and of the Duchess of Beja, who would have no more children, and he sent us greetings and encouraged us both. He wrote about Lisbon, which we wanted with ardour to see again, but had no way to do that. The Duke wrote beautifully; he did not go into too many details with regard to politics as he knew we were not interested in that. He also said he had sent us tea, for us to recall a bit of the flavor of home. Indeed, the Queen had received, from the Franciscans, enough for quite some time. He sent us a portrait of his heiress, a lovely young girl. I took the portrait, and I confess having kissed it.

"I have also done this dozens of times, Juliana," the sovereign told me, sighing. "I don't think like my mother, may God rest her soul in peace, who said that she would rather be a Queen for one day than a duchess for a whole life. I would give anything to be only *Infanta* Catarina and to live in the shadow of my brother, and maybe see you married with children."

"Catarina, you seem to forget that Gaspar was married, and yet I have never forgotten him. I still love him, and I always wake up in tears. Sometimes I just wish I could keep on sleeping, so that my dreams could bring him to me. It seems like only yesterday I was in your room and I exchanged the only kiss in my life. Look, I still wear his ring on my neck!"

"Do you know that he has been dead for some time now? I have kept this from you; I was afraid you would suffer. He did not have any children. He truly left his heart in Portugal and took yours with him to Spain. He passed away in 1667, it's been a while since then."

The Queen was telling me that *five* years later, after the duke had left this world. I felt the tears coming down my cheeks. I let them. What did it matter? It did not matter. We hugged and we mutually comforted each other. This life of mine did not matter at all; should I have passed away, what would I have left behind me? Nothing. At least Catarina's sister-in-law, Maria, had the inspiration to ask the Pope to cancel her unconsummated marriage to Alfonso, and Pedro immediately married her, thus saving her. How she could have been married to two brothers was something I could not understand; the Queen and I, we weren't granted anything. Even if I had remained home, I could not have loved anyone else. I was going to pray differently for my Spanish duke, who had found his peace away from me, in the burial chamber of the dukes of Medina Sidonia. The Queen understood me and respected my moment of silence, then went on:

"Do you know how I pity Alfonso?! God has always put truth in the madmen's mouths. I can still recall the departure to England. His laughter, which was meant to convey something to me.... Had I come down from the ship then...."

"You were already Queen. The contract had been signed," I reminded her. "There wasn't anything you could do about that, but I believe that those looks of his were a sign. The poor miserable man is suffering in Azore, while you are suffering here. You two are so much alike, only he is not lucid; he does not feel pain so vividly, while you are feeling it for yourself and him, too. Poor King, what has he ever done wrong to have such a life? But I think we shouldn't talk about him anymore. We should instead talk about that beautiful little Isabel! I would love to see her, to play with her in the wonderful sun of Lisbon. Here it's summer and it's cold. But there is no way to do that. We shall never see her! We shall only enjoy the portrait, and that will be it. I wonder how she

47

runs in the park, with her small, chubby legs? Who is taking care of her? Will she reign if your brother has no more children? It would be interesting to have a Queen on the throne of Portugal!"

"Last night, I dreamed about Anne, passed away so young," Catarina changed the subject. "Her father was screaming after her, but the duchess would not turn around; she could not hear the Lord.... Probably he was not allowed to attend her funeral.... But what a strange dream to have, just now! I'm sure clouds will gather again over us. The poor man, after having ruled England, is now living isolation across the Channel, and is mourning his pain by himself. It was as if I was on a road, and Anne was wearing a dress she wore at a ball. She seemed to be stumbling, with her eyes fixed straight ahead, and her father was chasing after her, but could not reach her, even though the Duchess of York could barely walk. I woke up and I could not go back to sleep after that, and I didn't want to call you either. I finally composed myself, and it was a good thing I did that. I think we have to be careful about everything moving around us. I don't think this is about another mistress; I'm already used to that," the Queen added.

And my dear Queen was right about that hunch. The King, advised by his beautiful mistress Louise, and bypassing the decision-making power of Parliament, adopted an ordinance stipulating that everybody had the right to practice his/her religion without being constrained in any way. Thus, a storm broke out with a violence hard to describe. All the members of Parliament, or better said, the Protestants, fought back with hatred over the King's action – he had no right to rule by means of ordinances. That statement set out the same rights for Catholics; their criminal proceedings were suspended, and above all, sustained the Catholic France. As a consequence of that Declaration, the King started the third war against the Dutch. The King wanted peace and he hoped there would be no further oppression of other religions.

Protestants responded vehemently, and the scandal could have had unexpected consequences. Parliament had had enough of the current favorite lady of the King, who was much more beautiful, but in particular, more intelligent than the ones before her. That woman had become quite costly for the English people. She shamelessly received expensive gifts, and which was worse, the Queen liked her. The war against the Dutch was not supported by the people, and when the King came out and stated his support of the French cause, the disaster was simply unimaginable, just as during the reign of Charles I. People shouted vehemently that the sovereign had overstepped his prerogatives, that he was not allowed to reign through ordinances that were not validated by the legislative forum.

48

He was reminded to his face of his father and of the exile he himself had to endure, and so, frightened and vacillating, the King withdrew that "Royal Declaration of Indulgence," thinking naively that the whole thing would end there. But the Anglicans were just getting started, as time would show us. They had come up with a plan whereby every man who held public office should state his religion. All the Catholic peers lost their offices, and even Barbara Villiers had to leave her position as a Lady of Honor to the Queen. Only Louise was left of the Catholic ladies in 1673.

Barbara left the palace and the King, drawn by new adventures. Of course she was still living separately from her husband who made no move to take her back. In truth, Barbara did not want a quiet life, with no fun and no lovers. After the Catholics left Parliament, that forum openly declared its opposition toward France and the alliance with that Catholic country. The Duke of York, the Catholic heir of his brother, who confessed his religious faith, also fell victim to that violent reaction. Hatred came down on the Queen as well, who could not present England with an Anglican heir. Nobody hoped for a miracle any longer, and the King was under pressure because of that situation, still refusing to divorce Catarina; on the contrary, a little girl was born, and he admitted to be her father. The English world had had enough of so many acknowledged children, but none of them suitable for the English throne.

And yet, the two deeds, "The Royal Declaration of Indulgence" and the requirement to state one's faith had another consequence, too, a political one that time. One of the most influential political leaders following Lord Hyde, namely Lord Clifford, only recently converted to Catholicism, had to withdraw from all his offices, and thus the power of his political group, known as the Cabal, diminished markedly. The Lord withdrew to the countryside to one of his domains, and soon after that, passed away.

But there is always a character just at the right place to eat from the corpse of previous rulers. The fall of the Cabal made room for the uprising of Lord Danby, an extremist and highly active Protestant who, starting in 1674, took power completely in his own hands. He refused to approve financial subsidies for the war against the Dutch, leaving the King too exhausted from so many conflicts, to effectively resolve that remaining conflict. Charles, peaceful by nature, did not understand the division among his own subjects, which was a reality of his reign. He was granted less and less money for his own living. His favorite, his dear Louise, spent most of her time at the Queen's apartment, where she felt safer. Charles had no more money to buy presents either, much less gifts for the Queen, who had forgotten when her husband last bought her anything.

I liked Louise for her clear mind and her warm beauty which charmed everyone. After Barbara left, she moved into her rooms, making the King wonder whom he did that for, himself or the Queen − both, I would think. We would sit and have tea with biscuits, and sometimes the King would find Louise in the Queen's apartment, and he would linger there over a cup of tea, and then they would leave together. Nothing disturbed Catarina anymore. She was just afraid for those having the same religion as we did. She had had enough of the Dutch and the shouting that there were too many of us gathered for the religious service held in the religious house, which had been built close to the palace. A fine place of entrapment, if one thinks about it. But fortunately the English did not think about it..

Also, the King's favorite encouraged us to attend balls and soirées with other "faces," for we did not have to wear a sad face, as she would put it. We had started wearing light colored clothing, impeccably tailored, according to the fashion at that time. We even danced, showing that we could enjoy ourselves. Sometimes it is a good thing to come out of one's secluded corner, to get some fresh air, to have something to tell afterward. We spoke perfect English, and we still had enviable figures. But those moments were few, yet we had them to relieve tension. We would also amuse ourselves at the expense of the flushed face of the Lord which would change color, showing us that sobriety was a good thing; of course, we forgot for a moment that since the Restoration, the word *morality* had been gone from the English dictionary.

The Duke of York had just brought a beautiful and agreeable bride whom we all liked. There were a few noteworthy moments in England's history at that time. Maria of Modena, who became Mary, was a perfect Catholic, though hated by the English. Everybody was afraid of a prospective Catholic son. Those island people had that constant obsession. Mary fitted perfectly in our quartet and exhibited much charm, especially when we all started speaking French over a cup of tea or during a walk.

CHAPTER 7

Mary tried hard to make herself loved by the English people, but in vain. Her husband was even more despised because he also had chosen a Catholic wife. That anxiety persisted, but since there were more of us, we would quickly forget about problems when we went to the countryside in the carriage. Sometimes we would wear different clothes from those we wore in the Court, and we felt wonderful. We could hear the soul of nature breathing in each being, in each plant, in anything that was alive around us. We liked listening to the wind blowing through the trees, the water flowing down the river, the little frogs jumping around, frightened if we came too near them. Our laughter would trigger the curiosity of the peasants who never dreamed of having the very Queen right before them. Sometimes our picnics would draw children together, and the Queen would fill them with food, especially sweets. They would stuff their mouths with all they could eat, then they would smile as a thank-you and run back to the field. They left us laughing and in a good mood.

From the very beginning, the life of the second wife of James had not been so bleak. We managed to make it easier for her, and there were four of us at Mass. The Catholic people from town would come to us, to the palace, to praise God, knowing that no one could touch the Queen and the new Duchess.

During that time, the King was caught, as usual, between the two religions; one was asking him for divorce, as well as an Anglican heir, while the other demanded the observance of their faith. Each of them had more and more demands and wishes to be fulfilled. Charles II had the disagreeable duty to make a decision. With the concern about his heir constantly on his mind, he decided to consult his brother one day when things were calm at the Court. He called his brother to his bedroom and told him about his plan:

"James, we have to marry my niece, Mary, to a Protestant, specifically William of Orange, which would put an end to the war because of which Parliament no longer gives us money – and in this way we also prove to be a quarter Protestant.

The King asked for his brother's opinion, pacing to and fro in his bedroom, under James's eyes, who had not thought of that. The Duke of York answered, after a moment of silence, that that was not such a bad idea, and that after he asked his daughter, they could start the process at the diplomatic level.

"Very well, my brother, you're saving me from big trouble. I have had enough of this, and I don't think I still have the power and the reserve I used to have to endure this religious atrocity. You know that we live almost entirely on what our cousin Louis is sending us. These crooks would let us starve. Go, hurry, ask her, but tell her we won't take a no for an answer; it's just a formal question, she has no choice."

"Then why ask her?" James inquired, astonished. "I will tell her that it has been decided and that is it."

The two brothers started to laugh, as they would seldom do in the presence of anyone else, but they could afford it then, for they were alone. There were few chances there for the walls to have ears.

Mary did not say no, and willing to begin a new life, she accepted the marriage; thus the talks began soon. She married in grand splendour in 1677 and thereby temporarily shut the mouths of Protestants, for she and her sister Anne were baptized in that religion, having Catholic parents, but being forced by the King to do so. I must tell you that Mary was only fifteen that year, only four years younger than her stepmother, but such differences and situations were common then. The two of them did not have much to say to each other. Unfortunately, Anne did not attend the ceremony on the 4th of November that year, for she was in bed with smallpox, and she was not allowed to leave her bedroom. She was only twelve then.

That marriage proved to be a happy one from the very beginning. They spent their first month together in England because they could not reach Hague. The cold weather prevented any ship from leaving the harbor. We knew they were expected, but what mattered for them was being together anywhere. They held hands and gazed into each other's eyes constantly, and their hearts were like two open books. Eventually, even the Duke of York was pleased by his brother's astuteness in choosing a husband for his niece. Mary was truly happy, and upon their departure, her husband mattered more to her than the family. William had completely conquered her, but he also fell into the net of love. According to their letters, they were impressed by the reception they got in the Netherlands.

Charles II was quite pleased. Things had turned out as well as they could for him; he had appeased the Dutch, and he made Mary happy. Then he could rest. At 47 years old, he wasn't young anymore, and his life of debauchery had left its traces. Catarina was 39, a mature age, and full of piety. That year, 1677, ended happily, with Charles hosting some magnificent balls at the end of the year, also attended by the Queen and her limited entourage.

The fireworks lit up the sky on New Year's Eve, and we watched them with delight. The King still had mistresses besides the favorite one, but nobody gave birth anymore. The last child, a girl called Lady Mary Tudor, had been born four years earlier. Thus the long series of children acknowledged by the sovereign ended. I believe that relieved Catarina a great deal. She no longer grieved her failure to carry a pregnancy until the end. It was God's will for the heir, that is the King's brother, to be a Catholic.

We had a lovely spring. When weather permitted, we learned to fish and we rediscovered the delight of taking our meals in the countryside, the smell of the grass, of the hay, but especially the quietness of the village. We learned to treasure and cherish each moment of stillness and calm which the Protestants' hatred had stolen from us. We would hear the birds in the trees quarrelling in noisy trills; we would hear life pulsing everywhere. We loved fishing and every catch was accompanied by a cry of joy. We liked the sensation of our fingers slipping down the fish, then we would throw them back into the water. Once we even roasted them on the embers. They were delicious. We had a wonderful time then. With outings like these, we had a lovely spring. Sometimes we would disguise ourselves as noblewomen and try to take the country's pulse ourselves, if I may say so. We discovered, in astonishment, that the peasants were not so vehemently against the Roman religion. They lived and thought much more simply, much closer to their beloved land. They were interested in being able to provide food for their families, in their agriculture, their numerous children, and of course the taxes that had multiplied since Lord Danby had settled in. I think this displeased them more than religion. I understood from this context that they were instigated to hatred. It was seldom that the few people ruling the Kingdom really did something for the lower classes. Better said, never did they do that. First of all, they were after their own interests and those of their friends; then "they'll see." Simple, ordinary people were useful for wars and taxes, but beyond that, they served no purpose. The rich men say: we live and die to rule, and when talking about ordinary people, they say: they live and die to defend me, my family, and my interests.

The Court at that time was full of ladies, and the detestable Lord Danby and his rancour, gained notoriety as a politician full of hatred. Everything was confused in the politics of those years, and I felt that something was terribly wrong, especially from the looks cast by the people of the Court toward the Queen. That Lord Danby was beyond everyone else. His full name was Thomas Osborne, Duke of Leeds and Peer of Carmarthen, holding the office of Secretary of State. He had made numerous enemies constantly contesting him because of the office he held. Each of them wanted to be his favorite, so that when he chose someone else, that person would shift sides, going to the enemy camp, thus breaking down the wall of the Lord's status brick by brick.

The first enemy he made was Charles Montagu, Count of Halifax, who hoped he would be assigned a high office in the Kingdom, which was granted, however, to William Temple, to the detriment of the Count. Thus a scandal broke out, with Charles Montagu accusing Lord Danby of having undertaken powers beyond his office, his title, matters of war and peace, of corruption, of theft from the public funds. The Lord was also declared anti-French.

The King also was exasperated with Lord Danby, while we had become invisible. We went each day to pray in the religious house next to the palace, there where all the Catholics willing to listen to the Mass and the word of God would come, to the aggravation of Lord Danby, who didn't look favorably on any crowd of Catholics gathered together. I could feel that he wished us evil, first of all to the Queen. We didn't go out anymore from the palace garden. We were, as they would put it, spied upon. But Louise de Kerouaille always succeeded in making us feel better. Whether she was a spy or not, we did not know, but during one of our walks, she made us understand that something serious was being plotted. We believed her, for she never told lies. We liked that she did not pay attention to the King's escapades with other women, and which was more, she was obedient to the sovereign, which made Catarina stronger and kept Charles under control. It didn't really matter whether men like Lord Danby, for instance, considered her a French spy planted by Louis XIV into the Court of England.

In late spring, a wonderful ball was thrown at the palace. The people had gotten rid of the Dutch, the weather was warmer, the days were longer, and the event was of good omen – at least that was what we

54

thought until Louise came over and whispered to us that there was always a storm following a too-brightly shining sun. Catarina turned pale when Louise hid that comment under a smile and a perfectly taken bow. Then, our happy mood spoiled, we withdrew from the ball, after the requisite time for the Queen to spend at such a gathering. We went upstairs to my apartment, where the Queen said, standing by the window:

"Juliana, what did Louise mean? What's waiting there for us?"

"I supposed nothing good," I said. "I believe Louise, she knows better than we do. She just wanted to warn you, that's all. There will be something, but I shall support you, and I hope that the King will do the same," I added in a low voice.

"Juliana, talk to me about our childhood. Where did it go, what's wrong with my life, what do I have to pay for, where did I go wrong? Why did my mother push me into this marriage? These political reasons make me so tired. I've had enough of this life. This year I turn 40, out of which sixteen years I have spent only in this ugly, ghostly palace. And so have you – 37 years old, and all your life has passed you by. The King is 48, but this is different for him. He is not like me. He is an Anglican Englishman. He's always taken life easy since the Restoration.

I've tried to ease her despair, doing what she told me to. I recalled, for God knows how many times, the childhood years, which, spent in the austerity of the monastery, were a true balm, given the situation we were in. We knew that Pedro was still Regent, and Alfonso was still the King, still exiled in Terceira. He was seriously ill and could not be taken to Lisbon. Maria Francisca had no more children, yet there remained Isabel Luisa, the little princess of Beira. She was already 9, and rumor had it that she was very beautiful. We did not know, though, whether she was already in the Monastery or had private tutors coming to the palace.

It was summer of 1678, and the sun was shining, burning us. We could feel the storm coming with every ray burning it all. Louise was right, something unpredicted was going to happen.

CHAPTER 8

Maybe you find this Queen's life monotonous, given the grayness of every day she lived in England. The recounting of this destiny is not exactly easy to do, and I can neither add humorous supplements nor embellish her story in any way. To a great extent, Catarina of Braganza's life was sad for more than one reason: a husband enchanted by other women, his incapacity to understand that all his affairs truly hurt the Queen, the desire for a heir, and speaking of that, the trauma of all her miscarriages. And last but not least, everybody's enmity toward her religion. I think that will do.

Maybe you wonder why I decided to tell the story of the one who had been my friend ever since we were just children at the monastery, knowing that not only spectacular things occurred. Maybe I would naturally answer you: because she had been a true friend, because there is not only joy in life, but also much frustration, helplessness, and pain, even for a Queen who normally would have received nothing but respect and obedience. If this Queen was to some extent left in peace, that was only when she didn't make an appearance, when she just remained secluded, disgusted by a Court that had reached the pinnacle of debauchery, making up, as it were, for the tranquility during the Republic. Theaters were full, women played their own roles in the Opera Houses, something unheard of before then, which thoroughly frightened and astonished us beyond any imaginable limit. Obviously, we seldom went to see those performances; we didn't like them.

Maybe it was the bad luck of the Stuarts that the Queen could not have children, but she paid for that misfortune, and she bore her cross with dignity, without lamentation, until her husband passed away a few years later, and we embarked upon the ship back to our Portugal. We were old, but we held a great desire to recover. Therefore, she carried her cross and she bore all the looks and all the insults laid upon her, knowing that there was an ointment for each wound in the world, which would later on heal her. That was the prayer that we always prayed in her private chapel. Sometimes, we just knelt down before Christ, searching for peace, without praying for anything in particular. So many times had she cried in my arms, afterwards becoming serene again. I also want to tell you that I have never considered myself inferior to her, even though she was the Queen, and I was a mere countess. Maybe we became closer also due to our situation. She needed faith and true love, and thank God, she had them all from me. She filled my heart, she filled up the space in my heart, together with her cousin Gaspar. The two of them shared that space. Gaspar – my first and only love, and Catarina – my first and only true friend, were my family.

But let's close the brackets on this explanation for those reading these lines. As a final comment, to me, the one who lived next to this woman, her destiny did not seem monotonous, but rather, comparable to the destiny of a butterfly that came too near the candle, and burning, she strove to survive and fly. Charles II and his brash Court were the candle to my dear Catarina. But her wounds will heal and she will defeat them all, by rediscovering her real self later on.

So we were in the year 1678, apparently a peaceful year, after the marriage of Mary to William. They had been living in the Netherlands for a long time, from where she sent us letters saying that she was happy and that her husband was everything she had dreamed of. William indeed loved the King's niece back, and they were hoping they would soon have a heir. The weather had gone bad in the middle of the year, and we had to remain in those rooms, which we did not like at all, in a boring, nun-like isolation. We expected the year would end just as dismally for us as had all the other years we had spent on that island with its unbearable climate.

Unfortunately, scandals resumed, not letting us linger for too long. Catarina, and I state this again, had many enemies who could hardly wait to "attack" her – everyone, starting with this Lord Danby, the one who actually ruled England. The only one who made a stand against him, with his stubbornness, was Charles, which the Protestants could not possibly understand. Few Catholics dared make an appearance at the Court; it would be reckless of them to do so. Chased, oppressed, killed or dragged through impossible trials, they preferred to move to the countryside to their domains and live in seclusion, never going out and waiting for better times for their religion. Thus, the hurricane that had started to come toward us took us by surprise, even though we had felt it in the air a long time before.

I think I should say no more, cut the story short, and tell you what Catarina, and Louise, a bit, too, went through – Louise who had remained a French spy in the eyes of the noblemen – and which also happened, just a little bit, to me, too.

A misfortunate, a lost man, a mean-spirited and duplicitous man thought, in his "devoutness" that it wouldn't be such a bad idea for the Queen to go back to her home, quickly, subsequent to a divorce, or, in the worst case, to be punished as an example. A man to whom the hatred toward the Catholic and childless Queen was a feast in his miserable life, a young man who had just turned 29, who could have thought about the life in front of him, plans, and other things of the kind, this man decided to say about Catarina that she was allegedly plotting against Charles. This man had the thought of scheming against the Queen to satisfy his inexplicable hatred against her. His scheme was called "the Popish Plot," in fact the presumed plot, and the goal of that dirty maneuvre was to remove the Queen, so that her husband could have Protestant children, namely Anglican heirs to the throne, with a much younger prospective wife. What he wished for Catarina was a trial, her dishonor, her exile, and any other things, each more terrible than the other.

Titus Oates, for that was the name of that man lost before God, was alternately a Jesuit and an Anglican priest; it seems he didn't know the path either, which was why he vascillated so much between the two religions, like a leaf in the wind. That "beetle," let's call him this, thought of staging an alleged Catholic conspiracy, in which of course the Queen was "allegedly" involved. In fact, that priest, if I can call that scoundrel a man of God, spread the rumor that Sir George Wakeman, the Queen's doctor, was conspiring with her to poison the King, everything being done (so he claimed) at the urging of my poor friend and with Catholic money.

The King, deeply shocked, did not believe a word of that scheme, but upon the request of Parliament, he consented to an investigation. That was all Lord Danby was waiting for. Thus, in the coming period, an anti-Catholic hysteria, unlike any seen before, arose. Many innocent people were killed in broad daylight, just because they were Catholic. Those innocent people did not know about the conspiracy; they were living hard, under the burden of the taxes set by the lord. That alleged conspiracy was a mere pretence, a match lit to inflame the Protestants. Corpses lay in the streets; fortunately, it was cold outside. No Protestant would touch them, for that would have defiled them, as they put it. Dozens of Catholics died. That winter was ugly and full of the darkness of the Protestants' sins.

Jurors had gone mad; judges passed sentences all over the country on the grounds of that plot, which the people knew nothing about. Lord Danby himself, who hated the Catholics and France as well, gave ear to Oates' lies. He strongly concurred that the Queen was involved in that conspiracy and he was rubbing his hands with delight, thinking that something terrible would now happen to the Queen, subsequent to that affair tainted with so much innocent blood.

Charles II, having had enough of the abjectness of that priest, evetually had him taken under arrest. He was weary of the cruelty happening all over the country. He vehemently defended the Queen in Parliament, informing its members, who had probably forgotten it, that he had been married since 1662, rather a long time. At the same time, he defended Catarina's doctor who, caught in the middle, was waiting to get back in peace to his business. But as the proverb goes, he was hoisted by his own petard, Lord Danby found himself accused by the Chamber of Commons of high treason and hostility against France, with the MPs exhausted by so many diplomatic wars during that time. The King wanted his cousin across the Channel to keep on sending him the sum of money set by that treaty, a sum attained with difficulty. The Lord accepted that, but he took it as a personal affront. Danby fell into the pit he had dug for the Queen when the Chamber of Commons determined that he was involved in a plot together with that miserable priest, and he was officially charged.

That turn of events also took the King by surprise; he found himself again in the position of having to choose, in that political maelstrom, between Danby and Parliament. He made the decision to save Danby, to acquit him, and at the same time to dissolve Parliament. That happened in January of 1679, just when I was privately celebrating my birthday at Catarina's with Louise, the Duchess of York, and our priests from Portugal.

The Queen complained that she was missing the advice given by Francisco de Mello, the former Portuguese ambassador to England, a wonderful man indeed, and a perfect Catholic. His mistake, for which he was repatriated, was to have published a book of Catholic learnings. As punishment, he was exiled from the England, and thus the Queen lost a true, wonderful, and especially devoted friend. We comforted her with the idea that at least he was not killed or punished in some other dreadful way.

My birthday was somewhat clouded by the terrible situation brought about by Titus Oates. It seemed the persecutions would never come to an end; we had one coming after another, and we were wondering how long we could endure. The King was irascible most of the time; he who was made for a life of personal pleasures had to spend his time mediating between the two constantly fighting religious factions, which found motives to fight out of the blue.

The next significant episode occurred in March, when the King himself was accused of gathering money for the Catholic cause, with a view to arming troops in order to quell the anti-Catholic hysteria, money doubtless coming from his French cousin. Caught in the middle again, Charles was forced to admit that the dissolution of Parliament and the acquittal had no influence whatsoever on the trial of Lord Danby. That lord, who found himself alone with no support, had to resign from the office he held, that is Secretary of State, and accept that the King's pardon had no effect on the Chamber of Commons. I am telling you these things not because we were connected to those unhappy situations, but because I just want to emphasize the times in which we lived.

The Queen watched, amazed, at how her husband stood up for her anywhere, in front of anybody, seemingly taking onto himself that hatred that we did not understand, but with which we had learned to live. Charles insisted loudly that his wife was incapable of such senselessness and demanded the same undying respect for her. Was he in love with her? Did he pity her? Nobody ever knew that, but Catarina loved him for certain. He had won her heart with his sustained devotion. She was grateful to him and would sometimes smile at him. If she was not happy, at least the Queen's heart was cosetted, for she knew the King would always defend her. He had always done so. On one of the visits of the sovereign, he proved to be more relaxed, finding the necessary manners to be kind to his wife, who took his hand, kissed it, and in tears, said fervently, "thank you." Charles did not expect such a manifestation of gratitude, but did not withdraw his hand ; on the contrary, he took the Queen's hands into his and held them for a few moments, as if Catarina had been a bad-tempered child who had to be mollified. We did not have many such moments during our stay on the island, but there were quite a few which I can still remember. The King waited for Catarina to recover her composure, then said goodbye, a bit troubled, as if he was discovering his wife for the first time. I think he spent that night with Louise, who was a lovely, very respectful and tactful lady. And yet, the Queen was not bothered by that situation.

We liked and accepted Louise. She had been just as terrorized, and involved as we were in the Popish Plot, as they called it. Her past was again ransacked, and she was considered to be Louis XIV's spy, but she had an unexpected ally: the Queen. If Charles defended Catarina, the latter defended good Louise. Louise always remained grateful to Catarina for that gesture. I believe that the King was grateful to his wife also because of her astute defense of his favorite. Who knows? Only her soul, gone to heaven for a long time now and our good God who accepted her confession on her dying bed, when nobody stood against her anymore, thus fulfilling her last wish. I remember those times, which I will talk about in the coming pages and at the right time. I remember that as if it had happened yesterday.

With the will of the good Virgin Mary, Catarina and the King's favorite survived that plot without being charged, but Lord Danby did not manage the same quiet moments. One day, Louise came quickly to see the Queen, for she, just as I, had the right to enter her room anytime, telling us the latest news. There had broken out out a dispute between the Chamber of Commons and the Chamber of Lords with regard to the punishment for Lord Danby. The Chamber of Lords was more moderate, if we may say that, and they wanted the former Secretary of State to be exiled wherever he chose. The Chamber of Commons intensely wanted him to go to prison. King Charles II was, as always, caught in the middle; he chose, somehow constrained, the worst punishment: imprisonment in the Tower of London. The sovereign was dissatisfied with that decision, but acquittal did not have any effect on the sentence, and Danby spent the next five years in the Tower, to the chagrin of his family.

You know how the audience watches from the theater boxes, with every spectator whispering and covering his or her mouth with the hand; that was very much what was going on in the Court of England at the time. Things were happening quickly, one right after another, but without the audience's applause. We did not have time to think; there was always something new being staged, drawing all of our attention. We could afford to watch because, thank God, Catarina was no longer burdened with those accusations; neither was Louise. The plot failed, but left deep traces in our consciousness. The Queen went to the special Masses for the poor, miserable people who were killed and for whom nothing could be done anymore. Her chapel was open to whomever wanted to pray. There were not many; because of fear, only a few came, but they all saw the lady dressed in drab clothes and covered with long, thick veils. They knew that in that secluded corner there was their miserable Queen.

It was with difficulty that we overcame that ordeal. The walks in the countryside helped us a bit to smooth our tired and aging foreheads. Our hair went gray thinking about what we had been through and what could have awaited us in that England full of the unpredictable. Catarina had no safety as Queen of the Protestant England, mainly because she was a practising Catholic. Those island inhabitants had had sovereigns

61

beheaded before; that would not have been anything new to anybody, but merely a new show on a London stage. I believe that the Queen had thought about that at least once, just as I had, but she never brought up the subject. It was frustrating when we learned that that schemer, the wicked Titus Oates, had been released, and to our astonishment, we ladies in the Queen's entourage, he was given a place to live in at Whitehall Palace. It was outrageous, but that was the decision that had been made, and we had to accept it. I was amazed by the courage that the Queen showed when she told me that she wanted to pay him a visit. There were only the two of us. The King had gone out for a walk with Louise.

"I want to look at him," Catarina said, "I want to see his eyes. I have to do this. Ever since this idea came into my mind, it has been haunting me."

I did not answer, for I knew I could not fight that, but I asked for permission to accompany her. She granted it, provided I said nothing. I agreed to that, for at least I was with her. We were still living at St. James, so we had to travel to Whitehall by carriage. It was not difficult to enter that priest's housing; nobody was watching his door We just had to ask where he lived, and after a bored "come in," we were admitted. The Queen lifted her thick veils and looked him in the eyes. I remained covered and mute, as I had promised. Oates recognized his mistress, and there was a moment of amazement, which he easily overcame, for one could see that he knew how to approach people. He began, to his shame, to blame it all on Danby, forgetting about the respect due to the Queen. It was a short meeting – how else could it have been – during which the rudeness of that man came out. The Queen let him talk and at the end, just uttered a sovereign "I forgive you!" Then we left, disgusted. I have no idea what Titus Oates felt afterwards. Those two words shocked him, for the forgiveness came from a true Christian. In the carriage, I promised the Queen that I would pray for his soul. She had decided to do that and asked me to utter the same prayers. I obeyed, but without conviction, may God forgive me for that!

I had received news from our warm country: I lost my parents, who had died in an accident. That news made me sad; actually, not the death itself made me sad – death is naturally part and parcel of man's life – but the terrible and painful way they had gone to eternal heaven. But what could I have done from a distance? I wrote back to my brothers, sympathizing with them and telling them that my heart was with them. I hoped I would see them once again before passing away, and kiss one more time the ground of the country where I first saw daylight.

On the other hand, King Alfonso lived. He clung to life every day; he was paralysed, but he was alive. Pedro was still Regent, and rumor had it he was unfaithful to Maria Francisca. She had never gotten pregnant again, the couple having only the little girl I told you about. Catarina thought her niece would take the throne some day. Was she going to be an *Infanta* of Portugal? Who could answer that? Time would tell with every day that passed by. *Infanta* was ten by then, and I doubt she was thinking for a second about becoming a Queen. I think, though, that she was enjoying childhood with her mother.

CHAPTER 9

Years went by, one after another, in this royal, long, and sterile marriage. Protestants were more and more certain of a Catholic succession to the English throne, for James was a practising Catholic together with his wife. So that English faction had no satisfaction. They didn't know where they could possibly have found a prince with the legitimate right to be a King.

Charles II was 49 in the year I am telling you about, so he was getting old, I would say. He had fathered enough children, but none of them was legitimate. He had been a woman-chaser of the first order, and he had naturally shared favors with duchesses and comedy actresses, as well as good-looking and well-built servants, but his children were not recognized as ascendants to the English throne; they were counts, dukes, or lords, but only created; none of them had any birthright to the titles.

If you remember that organization called Cabal, that was dismantled in 1673, after the King's failed Royal Declaration of Indulgence. Many of its members stepped aside, but there were also a few supporters who remained, waiting for the right moment to come back, especially when Lord Danby was imprisoned in the Tower of London against his will.

One of the former heads of that organization was also Baron Anthony Cooper, who thought that the moment was right to return to the political stage. Many of the Statesmen were having secret talks concerning the succession to the throne. They first mentioned the name of the King's first-born son, even though he was illegitimate; that was Lucy Walter's son, Duke of Monmouth. After much whispering behind closed doors, they had decided to take direct action. When the Chamber of Commons wanted to issue a deed whereby James would be excluded from his brother's succession, due to being Catholic, the storm strongly broke out.

Charles, by nature disinclined to get too involved in the ruling of the Kingdom, had literally put his hands on his head and found the simplest and easiest solution at hand, namely to dissolve Parliament for the second time. Fear made him take that course so that James, his legal heir, would not be excluded. When he first dissolved Parliament, he did it out of the desire to save Lord Danby, but that had no effect, and he hoped that that second dissolution would be fortuitous for James. He had had enough, and he took that action so as not to complicate things too much and to return soon to his peaceful, self-centered life. This is what was happening, if I remember correctly, in the summer of 1679. We had passed the first half of the year. Charles had taken that step truly thinking that the next Parliament would be a moderate one which would understand that the King had learned how to cooperate with the legislative body. Well, he was wrong again. There was a risk that the Exclusion Act would pass with that Parliament too, and James risked a great deal.

That Parliament resisted for too long, and Charles had learned to nonchalantly dissolve its two parts, which he did in 1680 and again with the next Parliament, which he dissolved in 1681. So he dissolved Parliament four times, to the bewilderment of its honorable members. We wondered how long he would go on playing with that new "toy," which terribly annoyed him and did not entertain him as any toy should do. Catarina was worried about so many dissolutions and re-elections, and dared to request a private meeting with the King in her apartment. There were just the two of them; I subsequently learned about that. Catarina, tears in her eyes, begged him to set her free, to divorce her.

"You could marry a young woman; you can still have children," said Catarina, wringing her hands. "I caused this situation. I could not bring a child into this world. I have had enough of so much trouble, so much hatred, and the Duke of York would be free with this solution, and he could find his peace."

"Madame," said Charles, "when I got married, I was old enough so I knew for certain what I was doing. I vehemently refuse to do that! I'm proud that you're thinking of England, but England is not thinking of you, so it is not worth doing! Your life has been a nightmare, and I don't care that I don't have legitimate children. I don't deny that there has been a time when I cared about that, and I suffered because of it, but as time goes by, I've become if not wiser, at least less impulsive. James will follow after me, and from that point on it will be his business. I don't care. I'm not coming back from the grave. Discussing succession is talking about my death."

As he spoke, Catarina cried harder. The King, drained by that speech, offered her his perfumed handkerchief, kissed her hand, and after bidding her goodbye, went out the door, leaving the Queen confused by that unexpected gesture Charles made to her. Catarina immediately came to see me and told me everything. She was holding the King's handerchief, which was then full of her tears.

"Juliana, I honestly don't understand anything anymore; if you understand something of this, please tell me."

"I think that the King is simply growing old," I answered, "and I also think he is doing this on purpose, to give Protestants one more slap. Also, I think he is right. Succession means his being dead. It is a shame that his whole reign comes down to this – either legitimate children or his brother. The King is a character who likes having fun, not what comes afterward, and I also think that it doesn't matter anymore so much that he does not have children with you; I don't think he lied to you, and I also think that you shouldn't bring this subject up for discussion anymore."

The Queen made me that promise and became peaceful. She had the handerchief given to her by the King, whom she loved with all her heart. She had given herself to him, and expected nothing in return, so she was feeding on gobbets. I guess the King had no idea about it.

Politically speaking, Charles was fortunate. The people were weary of his bestirring against the Catholics, and he did not want that exclusion. Logically, James was the legitimate successor to the current King. The people were touched by the two deaths in the new family of the Duke of York, even if they could not stand Mary. James was English, and he had lost two children. In that favorable context , Charles heartened and accused Anthony Cooper of treason, threatening him with a suit. Cooper quickly understood that his hope was lost, and taking his family, he went to the Netherlands, where he later became ill and died.

To ensure his peace, the King thought to rule the country without a legislative forum until his death. He had had enough of so many groundlessly inflamed Protestant minds. He was exhausted with crimes and pain and duality. During that time, we moved from St. James Palace to Whitehall. If one did not remember that Charles I had been executed right in front of the palace, it was more confortable than St. James, at least in terms of our apartments. The King took his wife on a tour of the building and showed her the apartment where he was born. Catarina wanted that apartment for herself. Charles did not object to her request. She even found it interesting and easy to move into. Nothing had changed; everything there was just as in his childhood. I liked it for a different reason: my apartment was next to the Queen's and connected with hers through an interior door.

"Juliana, this room makes me feel melancholic. I'm thinking of my husband as a small child, and of this bed where he was born. Henrietta Maria was blessed; she could give birth, but what is more, she gave birth to two boys, one who could follow the other to the throne."

All I could do was to embrace her, looking also at the bed where she would sleep. For as long as I stayed in that palace, it was calm in England, and most of the months passed by without our suffering too much, maybe only because of my hair turning more and more gray.

We were happy when God finally proved to be just, and the Protestants turned against Titus Oates, who ironically was living under the same roof with us. The world was tired of the Catholic blood flowing from the same England, and after Oliver Plunkett was injustly executed, William Scrogg, the minister of justice at that time, declared the Catholics innocent, without interference into the Popish Plot, and their trials ended.

The death of Oliver Plunkett, archbishop of Armagh, was the last of that long series, in terms of importance, significance, as well as rank of the unfortunate beheaded man. We prayed continually for this country, which was surviving the fight between the brothers living there. The King took advantage of the fact that the hatred had diminished and asked Oates to leave the palace. The latter stubbornly refused, to Charles's indignation – he was extremely sensitive and ill-tempered when it came to that subject. His nerves on edge, he accused Oates of sedition and of his denunciation of the Duke of York, and threw him into prison. The mark of the Popish Plot had shut his mouth, but his heart remained full of bitterness and hatred.

It was the summer of 1681. The King had passed the midpoint of his life; he was 51, and one could see that he was just as tired as we were. At that time, we could go out more often; it was safer in the streets, and the hatred was well concealed – in other words, subdued. Protestants accepted the situation of the succession, and Charles peacefully received the subsidies from his cousin. We even attended balls again, which by then had as guests Catholic lords returned from their domains hidden God knew where, in what corner of England. Mary de Modena was still grieving over her little girl. Louise remained with us; she was our friend, and she had a permanent apartment in Whitehall. How else? She put up with the King's escapades; he was also invigorated by the peace that seemed to last longer that time. She was still beautiful, and still the favorite. She still received expensive gifts from Charles, and of course, she was Duchess of

Portsmouth. She was 32 years old, and it seemed as if time had left no trace on her; she was just as fresh as when she first arrived at the Court of England. We liked her. Louise cheated on the Queen, and the temporary mistresses cheated on Louise, so everything balanced out. I think she encouraged Catarina, thanks to her self-confidence, inspiring that in the Queen as well.

No Parliament was convoked; the King ruled freely, and the Catholics could breathe easily again. This was how the next year, 1682, passed, with occasional skirmishes, but quietly, even though we all knew that behind any silence there was a mouth willing to talk. Life at Whitehall was truly pleasant, even if we often felt the tendency to watch out and look behind walls or around corners. We liked exploring the whole building, visiting the painting gallery, looking at the family portraits, watching the changing of the guards, going to the theater, and learning to enjoy life again. We were amazed, but thoroughly delighted at seeing Catarina's picture next to the King's. There were paintings from their youth, and the Queen was dressed lavishly in bright colors. As for Charles, it is well known that he was always dressed impeccably, perfumed, and displaying very good manners.

"Catarina," I told her, "you are the Queen of England, not just a tenant at Whitehall. They have forced you into a whole life terribly alone here, but this painting shows who you really are: the sovereign!"

"As if it all mattered, Juliana? I will never change my plain clothes. I am the Queen, but more as a formality. In fact, I am very inconspicuous, and I don't think I will change anything now. I don't think that this peace between religions will last too long, so we have to see what lies before us, so as to keep safe. I don't think the English people appreciate that good Charles is ruling the country without a Parliament. I have a feeling things won't remain this way for very long. I also think that the King knows this, but chooses to ignore it, as if it were an ugly thing demanding thought. Nothing is sure here. You will see that soon!"

CHAPTER 10

In the previous chapter, I mentioned the firstborn child of the King, namely the Duke of Monmouth, James Scott. He was 34 then, in 1683, so he was in the prime of his life. He was married to Anne Scott, a beauty of a woman, who had been his wife since 1663. They had seven children together, whom they could support.

The Duke was ambitious, and Cooper's failed idea stuck in his mind more than ever. "Why not?" he wondered. He didn't love his father at all, and he openly hated his Catholic uncle even more. In fact, the feelings between James and his nephew were mutual; the Duke of York had never believed him to be Charles's son, but the son of another lover of his mother, Lucy Walter, namely Colonel Robert Sidney. But the King acknowledged him, so the problem was thereby resolved. James Scott didn't care about his uncle's opinion, except that it bothered him sometimes.

That young man had a flock of supporters close to him, always around to flatter him. He was an influential man in certain political spheres, and the natural and spontaneous but illegitimate desire to rule pandered to his *amour propre*. He was a callous character with numerous mistresses and debaucherous parties. Forgive me for saying so, but he had someone to emulate. He was a lazy man in his own way, and the idea of being the King was driving him to distraction. He presently conceived of a plan whereby he could fulfill that great goal of his life. Only a few acquaintances faithful to him and greedy for power knew those plans, dreaming about the high offices and titles that the duke promised he would grant them, if, if, if....

It did not occur to the King or James to think of something like that, of an evil coming right from their own family, from the very first-born child whom they had ennobled long ago. They dedicated their time to hunting, horse races, banquets, walks in the air, and they enjoyed the silence and peace they had had since the Catholic issue was appeased and the country no longer had a Parliament.

Charles II was proud of his many important accomplishments, not only with the opening of theaters and the use of actresses replacing men in their own roles. He was the founder of the Royal Observatory and the Royal Society for science, where learned people, including Sir Isaac Newton, carried out their specific activity. Charles also ordered the Royal Hospital Chelsea to be built, a hospital where the aged or injured war veterans had a safe shelter and a hot meal. He liked the arts and sciences, and one would wonder when he even had time for parties and his mistresses. He took under his protective wing the man who rebuilt London after the great purifying fire, that is Sir Christopher Wren.

Catarina proved that she was right, however, about the fury of the Protestants who had held offices in the Parliament in the not-too-distant past. They were discontented with the way in which Charles made that decision to rule without a legislative forum, as if that were the natural and normal course of things. Thus, there were many of those who supported the Duke of Monmouth and who still believed in excluding James from the throne.

In the Duke's circle, all committed to that idea, there were among others, Arthur Capell, Earl of Essex, Algeron Sidney, and Lord William Russell. They knew that the two brothers, Charles and James, had as a means of entertainment the upcoming horse races in Newmarket. Conspirators met and chose the killers who, in exchange for a great sum of money, had to do their job on the King and his successor on the way back to London. Everything was in place and the mechanism was perfectly set, so as not to break on the day in question, but they forgot about and left out God. On the very night before they had to leave for the capital, the house where the two of them were accommodated took fire. The King and James decided to leave immediately, so much sooner, to London. The Protestants were not lucky that time either. The killers on the way had no one to kill, for the King and his suite had already passed a long time before. The duke and his cohorts were disappointed and took it as a sign of fate. God wanted a Catholic on the throne; God was Catholic, as they could see it.

Their disappointment turned to fear when the conspiracy was discovered. The rumors spread and finally reached them, but they also reached the King, who became furious. He trembled with anger, and nobody could stop him. The Duke of York heard about the involvement of Charles's first born child, the Duke of Monmouth, and told his brother. In

70

his extreme anger, the King sent the Earl of Essex, apparently less guilty, to the Tower of London, to keep company with Lord Danby, while Sydney and Russell were sentenced to death and executed for high treason.

Fate was kinder to the King's son, and he had time to escape to the Netherlands to the unfortunate Mary, who was going through the same ordeal as Catarina, having miscarriages and being unable to have a heir. Mary, however, had the full love of William of Orange.

Before ending the episode related to that treachery, I must mention something thoroughly horrendous. The angry King and the Duke of York, who had sworn that if he caught the treasonous son, would kill him as if he were a worm, decided that the Queen, Louise, and I should attend the beheading of Sydney and Russell. The Queen protested, and so did Louise. We had never seen anything like that before, but even with all the pleas, we were forced to attend the gruesome event. We covered our faces and did not dare to look – that was far too much for us. We watched as if through a fog as those two climbed the scaffold. Then we closed our eyes, and silently prayed, shivering. That was a terrible experience. We did not see, but we heard everything. The crowd was screaming and shouting, clapping when the head fell down into the basket and was showed around. The executioner showed the severed heads to the crowd making sure everybody saw. I confess that we left from there more dead than alive, and if I stay now and think about that event, I relive it as if it were again real. I can hear the axe, the screaming, the word "blood." But let's come back. I really don't like this page from my life in England. What is certain is that that was the last episode in which Protestants plotted against the King or James.

The heir acquired great influence on the Court and reclaimed his natural rights *de facto*, not just formally. The Catholic lords who were in the Tower of London were released, and life resumed its natural course.

I saw Catarina during those days, murmuring and breathing with relief that the King, who had never loved her, was alive, was living for everybody but her. So much devotion, so much blind, unshared love, what a large, forgiving heart! That was the Queen, and those were the qualities that Charles never saw.

We received from our sunny country the news of Pedro's coronation. Poor King Alfonso's affliction had ended. Before he died, he was completely paralysed. He had been brought to Lisbon, as it was his desire to die there, and nobody objected. It was early October when Catarina received the news and started crying over her brother, that brother whom I did not know well, and who saw the progress of his disease every single day. First in the legs, then seizures, and then temporary paralysis and partial paralysis with stronger seizures, and the dementia attacks; after that, continuous paralysis with increasingly frequent dementia episodes and few lucid moments. A tormented soul, he clung like ivy on the buildings walls. During the same time, we got some news about the new Queen as well. Maria Francisca was ill, and the doctors believed she would soon pass away. Charles's only comment in that respect was that we all die, and that soon, we will reach that moment. Brief, but true.

Catarina became very sad at the thought that Pedro would soon be all alone, with only his little girl, his only offspring. Early the next year, we got the news that Pedro was a widower. Maria passed away on Christmas day in 1683, a blessed period during the year. She was only 37. Their daughter, the Princess of Beira, had lost her mother at such a young age, for she was only fourteen at the time. She decided to go to the monastery to pursue her education and to weep for her mother, unseen by anyone. During our talks, I perceived her as impressed and lacking support. They said she was ravishingly beautiful. We were so curious about that! We knew that she would soon marry, and we thought that maybe she would come into a better life.

As for the rest of the year, 1684 was peaceful. Even the King seemed to have come back to his senses. His life, so agitated and so full of carousing, finally took its toll. He had grown tired. Parties had become rare, but we did not miss them. Maybe the members of the Court who enjoyed those things did. The King preferred the peace next to Louise, or he would have a cup of tea with the Queen, which happened quite seldom. He enjoyed having light conversations while drinking that hot and flavored potion.

The Queen would not throw any party on her birthday, but she held a private tea on that November day. Then, the King talked to his wife more than usual. It was as if he felt his strength had weakened, as if he had turned into someone completely different, and his wife felt that and had a chill of fright. She came to understand that Charles, who had never been artful with her, was saying goodbye. It was a happy observance thanks to the King's attitude toward Catarina, but unhappy because of the other messages going from one to the other, misunderstood or unnoticed. Louise did not feel anything, and the King realized, I believe, what kind of wife he had ignored his whole life, instead choosing women for their bodies and not for their hearts.

Indeed, that was the last birthday celebration for Catarina as Queen. Charles slowly declined, and died in early February, 1685. During his last days, he called the Queen to come to him, but she refused to see him, and sent me instead with a written message, which I read trembling.

Catarina asked him to forgive her for everything and apologized for her lack of charm, for her religion, and for the want of children. James was also there in the room while I read the letter. He seemed full of emotion and quite touched. In answer to Catarina's letter, Charles said in very emotional terms that if anyone should apologize, it was he for the life she had had with him.

It was also during those last days of the King that, to everyone's horror, he converted to Catholicism. That was a tribute given to his wife, a silent tribute that only the two of us (the Queen and I) understood. It had nothing to do with the promise made to his cousin Louis. Since he was a Catholic then, he wanted a modest funeral, somehow to absolve his sins. He was buried in Westminster Abbey in a crypt that had been prepared for some time. Few people accompanied him on his last journey. His wife, wearing black veils, was with me in the same carriage, and behind us came James II, next to his wife who was childless like Catarina. Both their children died, Isabel when she was five, and Charles, one month after he was born. James had two girls from Anne Hyde, so the succession was assured, and the people were pleased that the girls were Protestant.

It was like a curse, not having children. Mary in the Netherlands could not have children either. Her sister, Anne, had married two years before, to the Prince of Denmark, and their first child died at birth; at that time, Anne was expecting a baby.

I don't know how pleased James was to be the King, for he knew what he had to face, and he knew about the hatred against his religion. My dear Catarina was free at last; she was no longer the Queen. She had finally escaped all that.

Louise did not wish to attend the King's funeral on the 14th of February. She told him goodbye in her own way, and returned to France, tears in her eyes. If she had ever had a mission of espionage, that mission was over for certain. We kissed her goodbye forever on the 10th of February, before she left for Portsmouth. France opened its arms and waited for her. She promised she would write to us. King Louis XIV saluted the new Catholic King of England and the conversion of the late King to Catholicism.

The weather was dreary on that February day. It was cold and windy, rainy and foggy. There was no opulence in the convoy. The funeral procession was austere, unlike that King during his life. The Mass was a Catholic one, which Protestants endured under duress.

A few days later, Catarina went to the Abbey only with me, and kneeling before her husband's burial chamber, she cried bitter tears. This was her goodbye to him, unseen by anyone. She wasn't Queen anymore, and that was the last time she ever cried over Charles II, and also the last time she paid him a visit. A chapter had ended; a new one was opening before her, but she accepted her destiny as "come what may," and not necessarily what she might want or hope for. She had to live until God called her to Himself.

CHAPTER 11

So Catarina was no longer the Queen, but she became the widow of the late King Charles II. That status afforded us more peace and apparently more safety. My dear friend was no longer obliged to see anyone, to attend various compulsory gatherings or meetings, or maintain a sovereign demeanor, which I am afraid she had never had and which had never suited her anyway. James II, the former Duke of York, was a Catholic, and the madness of ruling a Protestant country was now his. His wife, Mary of Modena, was unhappy; her two children had died long ago, but time had not erased their memory, especially of that little girl who lived for a few years. Anxiety spread among the English people when the little boy died only a month after his birth. What a relief for some people, however, among whom were the daughters of Anne Hyde. Mary had never gotten pregnant again after those sad events in her family life. She was a Queen detested by her subjects. She had tried to make herself liked by the people, but had no chance. She was a Catholic, and that said everything about her, irrespective of her merits. The English are a strange people – that was my impression until the end of my stay there.

Catarina wanted to move from the palace where she lived next to her husband during his last days. I know she had a discussion with the new King and his wife, who insisted upon having her with them, but the former Queen refused them and did not change her mind.

"I just want to withdraw to some quiet, pleasant house," she told them. "I want only the bare necessities for myself and Juliana. If that house had also a park, that would be wonderful. I don't want to be a burden on this State. This Parliament will always disapprove of anything extravagant. Anyway, you will already have to fight with them more than your brother Charles did; you don't need an extra stone to carry. I am telling you this from experience. I was a Queen for so long, and the stress became unbearable. You have to let me go, but not too far away. You won't see me so often, as I won't go out so much anymore."

"Let me think about it," James said. "I will arrange something as quickly as possible and you will soon be able to move in."

"Thank you, my brother-in-law," Catarina said. "I wish I could comfort you, Mary, but I am tired of seeing so many faces, one more threatening and malevolent than the other."

I was happy to learn that we could at last find our own peace. That was all we wanted. I think that only one or two days later, James gave us the housing he had decided upon. The servants were already preparing two apartments as well as rooms for those coming with us. Our new home was Somerset House, the house that belonged to the Duke of Somerset before it was seized by the King. That man was executed on Tower Hill. We had lived there before, temporarily, but then it had appeared in a bleaker light. Maybe it was because the image of the duke would come before our eyes more often. We knew from the painting in one of the salons that the man seemed to have been really proud of his status, which eventually brought him to his knees. We had no idea whether there was still anyone left from his family, for that duke was executed in 1552.

When everything was set, we moved in, in the most unspoiled quietness. It was perfect. Everything was modestly decorated but full of warmth. We thanked the King in a letter and we settled into our hermitage. Somerset House had a view of the Thames, an attractive, orderly park, and on the same land, there was a small cemetery with stone benches and old trees. We decided to take care of that small burial ground, and that made us happy and helped us pass the time, for we were doing something good. We had only Catholic servants, not too many of them, but enough for two ladies.

In April, in the same year as Charles II's death, we attended the coronation, but we stayed withdrawn and unobtrusive to the other guests. Who cared about a former Queen? It was a grandiose ceremony, and somewhat tiring, so we could barely wait to get back home, through the back door. It was not a joyful coronation; everyone was reserved, and we all knew why.

We received a letter from Portugal, in which King Pedro II urged Catarina to go back home, saying he was sorry for the loss of her husband. Catarina gladly answered him, telling him where we were living then and that we were sheltered: "My dear brother, my heart is telling me that this is not the right time for me to head onto the sea toward home. Something tells me to stay here awhile longer, and when I feel it is time, I hope they

76

will provide me with a ship, if only because I was the Queen once for so long, and I shall sail and come to die on the ground where I was born." Catarina also wrote to him about the difficulties of James's reign, which she thought would be brief.

I would like to recall an event that occurred during the first year of James's reign. Something astonished us, and there was nothing we could do about it except watch. We were out of the public eye, but news circulated and reached us, or servants would tell us, , or we would simply hear it if we were standing by an open window. Now let me bring the subject before you, as mentioned.

This concerns the Duke of Monmouth, the first-born child of Charles II, who had escaped to the Netherlands after that failed plot. Maybe he would have stayed peacefully there; maybe his life would have passed safely and easily, but the desire to rule, an obsession of his, did not leave him in peace. So he decided to reclaim his actually nonexistent rights. He gathered a small army and set off to dethrone James, the new King. James, who had sworn he would get revenge after the happening in Newmarket, could barely wait for such an occasion. The two men full of hatred for each other faced off directly in Sedgemoor, during the battle on the 6th of July, 1685. No matter how Catholic the King might have been, he was the sovereign and easily defeated the duke. I still cannot understand why he organized that rebellion, having such modest resources, and where his mind was, to have such poor thinking and reasoning.

James brought him to London and after a short trial, ordered him beheaded. Catarina intervened for the only time in her life, but with no success. The King reminded her, pointedly, of everything that Monmouth had plotted and that now, since he was in James's hands, it would be a mistake not to execute him. Catarina insisted that he was half Charles's flesh and blood, but her pleas were not heard. The duke was executed even though the former Queen had asked for life imprisonment. Of course we did not take part in that obvious revenge, which satisfied the new King, but brought on him the animosity of Protestants. The Parliament was a thorn in James's side, opposing everything he wanted to do. The new King was an advocate of religious freedom; he wanted all the existing confessions to survive in peace, for all their members were brothers, namely English. He also admired the way in which his cousin ruled France, and he would have liked to be able to rule England the same way.

The Anglican Church was irritated that she would lose supremacy in favor of the Catholic Church on her own territory. In fact, the whole three-year reign of this King was a battle between religions, with the Parliament, which was on any side but the sovereign's.

During the same period, from a corner of England, an old acquaintance of ours, the Catholic Roger Palmer, came back "on stage." He was appointed Ambassador of the Catholic England to the Vatican. He did nothing outstanding there, except maybe to exhibit the patience with which he endured the scorn of his compatriots, and in no small part, thanks to his wife whom I suppose you have not forgotten. We certainly did not. He was considered the biggest cuckold of Europe. He was ridiculed everywhere he went, but he would not divorce his wife. He kept Barbara joined to him, like a punishment. He was stubborn like the former King, and persisted in his decision to remain married to Barbara. That did not mean that his lady was then exactly unblemished. Consolations in other knights' arms came in a stream, to everyone's amusement. That was also around 1686, because that reminds me of the unfortunate Mary of Modena, the Queen of the English. She still hoped she could produce an heir, after the two tragedies in her life. James had two daughters, so that was some comfort to him. It was not Isabel's and Charles's fault that they died, but something hurt her. They were obviously a very devoted couple who loved each other, but Mary wanted a baby only for herself, and not for the English throne. I believe she was very much hurt by the Protestants' joy that she could not have a son and that her little boy, Charles, had died so long ago.

Those people still hoped for the arrival of James's first daughter from the Netherlands to rule the country. Mary could not have any more children, as I had previously stated. That was the thorn in her heart, the thing that troubled her mind, no matter how comforting her husband might have been. James's second daughter, Anna, enjoyed maternity, having a little girl, who unfortunately passed away the following year. That was truly a cursed family, with impure blood, whose women could not bring children to the world, much to their unhappiness.

This last subject was full of unhappiness, so we will leave it aside, and we will deal with the next year of James's reign, i.e. 1687. James was nothing like his brother. Charles was like a fish easily slipping through any kind of waters, whether troubled by storms or full of mud. James was a weak man whom the Parliament dominated. He never had the power to dissolve it; he did not have the ability that Charles II had so naturally developed. Because of that, his reign was short, for he could not foresee the subversive desires of the Parliamentarians, who were openly supportive, but plotting behind the King's back to dethrone him and bring Mary from the Netherlands.

The same year, we received news of Pedro's second marriage. His young lady was Maria Sofia, palatine princess. She was only three years

78

older than *Infanta* Isabela Louisa. Pedro got married to have other children, too. *Infanta* was not an energetic person, but rather sickly. She was beautiful indeed, but that was of no use to her. She was the most often proposed to and engaged young lady of those times, but none of those promises ever led to a marriage. In her life, she was engaged at least five times, but with no good ending. The princess of Beira was courted by the most important young men at that time: Victor Amadeus II of Savoia, Gian Gaston de Medici, the Great Dauphin of France, Charles II of Spain, and the Duke of Parma.

When Pedro married Maria Sofia, only Louis XIV was a bit dissatisfied, but that passed quickly, for the King wanted a French princess to be Pedro's wife in Portugal. Catarina was pleased and wished him happiness and many healthy children to save the Braganza house. She also hoped that her niece would marry a young man meeting her standards, for she was far too beautiful to be unhappy.

I mentioned earlier about how short James's reign was. Perhaps he would not have abdicated by force if the Queen had not announced the birth of a boy in early summer of 1688. That announcement crushed even the last bit of forced silence reigning over the legislative forum and the whole of England. That birth represented the fall of the Protestant Church and a Catholic successor to the throne. That child outlived his brother Charles; he even outlived the previous monarchs.

We were happy and wanted to congratulate Mary. That child offered a chance for them, but few people saw that. Anne had lost her little girl, as mentioned, and he was the only boy of the Stuarts. His biggest issue was his Catholic religion, which was a disastrous flaw at that time. Nobody acknowledged him, neither the Church nor Parliament. People even insisted that Mary had not been pregnant, or that she had had a still-born child and exchanged him with another baby. Under such wide protest, James had to convoke Parliament to inform and convince the lords that he was indeed the father of that child, that that was his child and therefore his successor to the throne. The daughters of James also got involved in that affair, with unapprehended passion; they were too on the conspirators' side, saying that that child had no right to the English throne.

James did not manage to convince anyone with his plea; on the contrary, the Whigs brought Mary from the Netherlands to England, together with protestant William of Orange, forcing the King to abdicate in favor of his first-born child. All of that undertaking, all of that action that the English are so proud of was called the "Glorious Revolution," whereby they abolished the Catholics on the throne. What I may note, as a passive witness of what happened then, was the surprise in relation to Mary's

79

attitude toward her father. She was arrogant, she lacked clemency. She was a callous woman, forgetting where she came from. When they arrived from the Netherlands, the people acclaimed and cheered them, completely forgetting about James. He had fled to Ireland, leaving his dear Mary of Modena to cross the channel together with their little boy. Louis received them, providing them with a home, from all his heart, and condemning that absurd revolution. Mary lived in Saint-Germain-en Laye until she died, waiting for her husband's arrival or the invitation to return to England, if James's partisan plans had succeeded.

William III and Mary II and were crowned as King and Queen and in January of 1689, and that could be felt even in our circumstances. Somerset House started to deteriorate, and the new monarchs paid no attention to a house they no longer used. The era of decline started with that. The park no longer had the pathways aligned. Grass was growing everywhere, the cemetery was so sad and neglected, but we would take care of it from time to time, for lack of anything else to do. London's gray left its traces everywhere. The green moss spread all over the building, the burial stones, the bench on which we were sitting, virtually everywhere. It was an ugly period seemingly from a ghost story. If a window broke, nobody took care of replacing it; only our servants, prisoners with us, would cover it with whatever they could find.

The action in Ireland of the dethroned King had no success. He was defeated by the new King in the summer of the following year and he was exiled to France. We never got the chance to see him again. I know only that Mary had one more baby, a little girl. They were accommodated in their cousin's house until they died.

What was interesting was the choice of the new King and Queen not to banish us two; we seemed to have been forgotten in that deserted house. Perhaps we were too insignificant and from a forgotten era, even if only five years had passed since Queen Mary II's death. Well, we would never make an appearance anyway. We were living as in a monastery. Sometimes we would imagine we were children again, happy in our flower garden and enjoying the peace of the small cemetery, which had become our friend and did not unnerve us at all anymore. We were living unnoticed, living our days in complete peace.

CHAPTER 12

Let's come back now to Mary II of England. She seemed to be made up of two parts, the first one who remorselessly humiliated and doomed her father, supported by the radical Whigs, the part that entered England proud and with her head held high – and then the opposite part that belonged to her husband.

In fact, that is not the right comparison; the first part of her character lies somewhere else. After they were crowned King and Queen of the Kingdom, Mary no longer wanted to rule, but chose to stay in the shadow of her husband who ruled almost by himself. That is the contradiction: she fought against James, but then, when she became Queen, she interfered only where it was compulsory for her to do so and where her presence was mandatory, especially with her direct involvement. She led the country only when her beloved husband was in military campaigns or was busy with other things. She was only 28 when she acceded to the throne amid the curses of her father, but she had the love of her husband, who loved her until death, as they swore they would do when they married.

Unfortunately, she could not have children, but she was beautiful, at least she always seemed so to me, surpassing by far her sister Anne, who had several miscarriages before she finally became a mother in the summer of 1689. They all were anxious about that beloved child, for whom both sisters had high hopes for the very life of the Stuarts. He had survived his first year by a miracle, to the wonder of all the doctors. He had an unusually large head for his small body. Doctors said he allegedly was hydrocephalic, and did not give him hopes of survival. But he was so loved, and love gives one faith for the better. He was appointed Duke of Gloucester. After those pregnancies, Anne put on a lot of weight, failing to regain the thin waist that Mary still had. Her husband, George of Denmark, still loved her just as much. Both sisters had been most fortunate in that respect, for they had loyal husbands with different occupations, none of which had involved women, though, as had been the case with Catarina de Braganza's husband. Charles II loved enjoying pleasures in comfort, in quietness, but he was very artful in surviving politically in order to satisfy those pleasures. I still wonder how his cousin Louis sent him that annuity without asking too many questions. But that is already history.

Sometimes I would receive a letter from France, from Mary de Modena. She expressed her gratitude toward Louis, who had been so good to her family, generously supporting her. She told us that she could pray at ease and go to church, for the palace had a lovely chapel. What bothered her was her husband James's state of mind, for he was truly tormented by having been dethroned by his arrogant daughter. He could not come to terms with that thought. He suffered tremendously because of that. She could hear him talking in his study, where he would sequester himself every time he felt the need to speak of his exile. Sometimes she would find him sitting on a bench with James Francis, explaining to the little boy who he was, and the poor child just listened to him and looked at him with his big, beautiful eyes. That child should have been the King; he should have been "King James," but one cannot fight politicians, irrespective of the King you are. Mary adapted to the idea of exile; she had found peace in her prayers before the Catholic altar.

Now coming back to our life in Somerset House, at first, as I recalled before, we were left alone. But we soon received an official letter, cold and deferential, in which we were informed of the cuts in the budget related to servants, and everything pertaining to our living, so that we were no longer allowed to have too many Catholic attendants. We were further requested not to complain to Parliament about that and to content ourselves with what we had. We did not have a very large staff, anyway, and Mary knew that. It was just a chicanery. We did not react to those restrictions; we replied that we would humbly obey the desires of our masters.

That happened at a time when Pedro II attended what he had foreseen a long time ago: Isabela Louise dying from chickenpox. Her weakened body was no longer able to cope with that ugly disease. We were sad because we did not get the chance to truly know that beautiful girl.

The second child of Catarina's brother was living, however; he was already one year old and in good health. Pedro was optimistic. He hoped the child would be his heir one day. He was born the same year as the Duke of Gloucester.

We became even more secluded, we endured, and we limited ourselves to two female servants and two male servants. We didn't even leave the house anymore, out of fear. The palace was so big and empty, as well as shabby and uncared-for. One could tell that we lived there out of pity. We had food, firewood and very little for our own expenses, but we didn't even need that. We could see the Thames from Somerset House, and we were thinking that everything would pass, just like the waters of that beautiful, wide river. We would go for a walk in the small cemetery, which was very neglected during those days. Sometimes we would receive news from "outside." One such message was that Palmer had been released on bail from the Tower of London. He left that place after sixteen months of suffering, to a domain in the countryside, and after that we didn't hear any more about him. That is what my friend started telling me about during one of our strolls on the park walkways, which we could barely distinguish. Grass was growing up everywhere, and ivy had covered the trunks of the trees, killing them slowly.

"Juliana," Catarina began, "do you remember when my brother asked me – in fact, advised me – after my husband's death, to come back home, and I said that it was not yet time?"

I answered that I remembered that, and I let her proceed:

"I feel that that time has come. Everything is going to fall apart here. The Stuarts are going to go soon, you'll see. Had I felt it then, I could have seen my niece and nephew who are gone now, and I regret that. I miss my family and a church where I can freely pray. Nothing is keeping me here anymore, except the grave of a man whom I never understood, but whom I loved as he showed himself to me. I'm tired. I feel exiled! Perhaps if I had had children, I would have had a mission in this country, but as this is not the case, I have made up my mind. Look what they did to James! Look at the desolation and wilderness everything around us is turning into! Mary does not have any children, and I think this is her father's curse there. Anne has the unhappy, hideous prince, with that strange deformation, whom I don't think will survive, no matter how much care he gets. This is the seventh pregnancy of this woman, and look what came of it! I don't think he will be the one to save the Stuart house. He is two years old, and I'm not sure this is a miracle, the fact that he has lived so long. I shall write an official letter, Juliana, and I shall ask for a hearing, which she will agree to, as I am her aunt. I shall do this soon."

My first gesture was to embrace Catarina and to try and contain my tears, but I could not.

"You've been waiting for a long time for me to talk to you about my decision, haven't you? You've followed me all my life; you've been a good advisor, as I have found with difficulty. You poor thing! Forgive me," Catarina said to me.

"Yes, I've been waiting for a long time, especially since the Queen's letter came. I felt I was suffocating; then I have grown old, and I want to die in my own country. I have my inheritance waiting for me, plus many memories, enough for a lifetime."

"Juliana, you will live with me, and you will move to live in the house inherited from your mother, the Countess, after I die, you promise?"

I made that promise to Catarina. What else could I have done? We were like two abandoned sisters in this world, used to living together, to bearing difficulties together, sharing sorrow and pain, as well as rare joys in life. We had reached the point where we understood each other with just a glance. I told her then that I would write to Pedro, that I would send a letter to my brothers, for them to know about my intentions.

"I'm happy, Catarina. This is a new beginning," I told her, sitting down on the mossy-green stone bench, "although I'll miss this rainy and foggy England. This is our youth we're talking about. We lived it here, even if my hopes died when your marriage contract was signed."

"Gaspar? You still have his ring," Catarina said, looking at my neck. "He's been dead for some time now. No children. In Spain. Maybe we'll go on a pilgrimage there. We will be allowed to, for certain. If you want to, I promise you we will go there. You deserve to kneel down before the grave of the man who stole your heart."

I kissed her hand, as a sign that I did want that, and that I was already dreaming about that moment.

"Then, Juliana, let's make some plans and dreams. I am writing the letter right now, and the Queen shall soon see us. Now let's go. It's too chilly and damp."

The next day, the Queen read the letter. Catarina hid nothing; she told her about her plan and her desire to gain a hearing. Mary was in the position of doing two good things for herself: getting rid of Catarina by sending her home, and shutting down Somerset house, but especially she would rid herself of a Catholic. She immediately replied to my friend, and even set a date. One could see from the letter her impatience to see us gone, and she promised that she would provide us with a ship and a crew when the time was right for us to go or whenever we decided upon leaving. She had set the hearing for late September, 1691; that was almost immediately after Catarina sent her the letter.

"She wants to get rid of us," Catarina laughed, reading her answer. "And we want to get rid of her, but we won't tell her that, so as to hasten our departure. I can't wait for us to leave!" said the former Queen.

I was happy, too, and I slept like a baby, even though I hadn't been one for a long time. Indeed, Queen Mary II took care of the entire schedule on the day in question. She sent us a coach with the insignia of Charles II, and Catarina noticed that it was the same coach that took us when we first reached London from Portsmouth. She recognized the upholstery because she had used it before during her reign. The royal coach was accompanied by butlers dressed in the colors of the Stuart house. Everything contrasted powerfully with our modest life in Somerset House, but I completely understood the Queen: she wanted to appear in the public eye to be on very good terms with her in-laws and somehow wanted to show the respect due to her uncle. I don't know how she handled the respect due to James II, her father, but she worked magic with us.

Actually, we were second to none; we dressed as if we were in the Court, which Mary appreciated – she was probably afraid that we would show up like beggars or some poor disinherited women. We put on the simple jewels we had, to which Catarina added the jewels of the House of Braganza. We looked as if we lived in luxury and richness, but only God knew how much effort we had made for that.

I did not attend that meeting. Queen Mary wanted to be left alone with the former sovereign. What I will tell you is what Catarina told me on our way back. Their meeting did not last too long, and I know only that Mary II was obviously thankful about our desire to leave. Better said, her eyes shouted that we had made the decision a little bit too late, but nevertheless, she provided us with a ship for the next spring, specially equipped for a Queen of England. They had also talked about children, and Mary said to her:

"Dear aunt, we are so much alike. Neither of us could have children, and my sister will follow me on the throne, for certain. What differentiates us is that William loves me, and accepted this miserable situation. Despite all this, I think that Uncle Charles, although he may not have loved you, felt something for you, something I cannot describe. When anything came up against you, he stood up for you like a titan, which speaks a great deal. I recall how many times he demanded respect for his wife. And there is one more thing I wish to say to you. I don't think the Duke of Gloucester will survive. God knows how much we all love him, how much care we give him to live, but I fear that all this is in vain. The Stuart House – whether Catholic or Protestant – shall die. I know that there is one more offspring of my father in France, but there is no chance for us to go back to Catholicism. Sometimes I wonder what would have happened if he had reigned? Would the Stuart House have gone on? Possibly, but this is a thought that I chase away. I'm telling you all this, aunt, because you will go away, and you won't be able anymore to influence England in any way. In fact, you have never interfered; you've just prayed, and that was all. I'm glad I won't live to see the death of the Stuart House. I will be gone by then."

After that monologue during which Mary could afford to be honest, she promised Catarina once again that everything would be prepared and ready after the winter passed, and their meeting ended there. That was the last time the two of them met, but that didn't matter to either of them.

Catarina, having already gotten a plan, wrote to her brother in Portugal. He replied to her, satisfied, saying he was waiting for her whenever she wanted to come, just to let him know some time in advance. He also said that his heir was healthy and strong, and that he was already two years old. He added in his letter to her some good thoughts from his wife Maria Sofia, who seemed to be pleasant and kind, and could hardly wait to meet her sister-in-law, who had been the Queen of England for so long.

We spent all winter making preparations; we spent the holidays in peace and quiet, with a meal a bit richer thanks to the calculated generosity of Mary II. We took with us the gifts of our King, presents, a few small paintings, things that were close to our hearts. We still had enough clothes to pack, plus other trifles necessary to a woman. We gave up a lot of things, because we did not want to load too many chests. Catarina had some jewels that she had received on her honeymoon, which she kept to herself, not giving them to the Crown treasury. Nobody knew about them, so we had all reason to believe we would reach Portugal with them. With every passing day, we quivered in anticipation like the waters of the Thames under our windows. My brothers had received my letter, which I had put in the same envelope as Catarina's. They expected me as if I were coming back from another world. They had prepared the house that belonged to me then, and they were waiting for me, especially my nephews, for whom I had bought several small gifts.

When March came, the Queen wrote her goodbye letter to us, also confirming the date of our departure to Portsmouth, details about the ship, the coach, and other things she had personally taken care of. Catarina thanked her profusely and told her goodbye, wishing a long life to the Duke of Gloucester, the last male offspring of the Stuarts, who stood a chance to succeed to the throne.

At the end of the month, in a two-coach procession, we travelled to the harbor in question, where our ship was waiting for us. We were alone in the front coach, and behind us came Marisa, our old servant, who had come with us to England, and with whom we were now returning. The carriages were full of our tightly tied chests which the modestly dressed butlers took care of, for security. On our way toward Portsmouth, Catarina talked continuously, remembering places and people and her husband.

"Do you remember, Juliana," she told me, smiling a little, "how long I waited for my husband in the city, after our arrival? A whole week. It was also there that I got married in two different religions. I think he was late because Barbara was expecting. But that is all water under the bridge now. I don't think about those things anymore, and they don't hurt me anymore either. We are going home. Anyway, we will always receive news from our Ambassador here, from London. He promised me that, and he promised to write to me. I'm really curious about this twisting of Stuart Kings."

It had started raining over the fields beaten by those merciless winds. We kept silent for a while, listening to the rain.

"I think Marisa is happy," I began, breaking the silence. "She came to my room and told me that. She is happy because she is going home and because she will die in her native land."

"Poor woman, all that she put up with for me and our religion," Catarina said. "But no more. It's over. We will soon reach Portsmouth. The exile is over. I think we deserve to live these last years of our lives in peace. This year, 1692, is a new beginning for us. We are going back "HOME." That is essentially what England meant for us, and it had finally ended thirty years later.

We travelled safely to Lisbon. Our ship was solid and well made. We had no storms and no major incidents. We were eager; we could hardly keep from asking the English captain several times a day when we would arrive. He displayed a detached attitude, the attitude of a man who was simply doing his duty, and we were too proud to talk to him very much. We learned with amusement that Marisa did not spare him, and after half of the journey, we were also informed as to how much longer before our arrival. We were counting the hours and the days, and it seemed we would never get there. Marisa was serving us both then, but she was happy, for she was sailing. And so were we. When we saw the coast of Portugal, we cried like two children, holding each other in our arms. We had arrived safely. We knew we would be welcomed by the King's entourage and by my brothers.

CHAPTER 13

It took us several more hours – it seemed almost as long as the bleak days we lived in England – before we reached Lisbon. Sometimes it seemed that we stood still, and we were watching the captain steering the ship, who remained oblivious. The English have a way of grating on your nerves without even uttering a single word. An icy look of theirs is worse than a cold rain.

The captain's annoyance seemed to grow with every inch of the way. When I saw the harbor from a distance, and sometime later, the midgets turning into people as we came closer, both our hearts and time stood still. We were home after so long, drained of life, exhausted, but on our dear land.

"God did not let us die on that island, Juliana," Catarina told me, taking my hand.

I agreed, tears in my eyes, especially since she spoke in Portuguese. What I felt then is hard to describe; it was immeasurable bliss. I was close to fainting. We clung to the balustrade, Marisa next to us, sobbing. We three exiled women were coming back home. Everything seemed to brighten, especially since it was hot and sunny. No cloud in the sky and no fog. We would not be chilled to the bone anymore for as long as we lived.

The closer we got, the clearer we heard the welcoming cheers, which astonished and thrilled us. When the ship docked, Pedro the King, together with my brothers, came aboard without waiting for us to come down. My brothers looked like my father, as I remembered him upon my leaving for England. Life had left its traces on them, abundant, but brief and over. Pedro was a bit younger, but I no longer found the child I had left behind.

We all embraced, overjoyed that we were together again. It was a truly happy moment, which I shall preserve in my heart forever. We disembarked, and on the shore, the Portuguese Court together with Queen Maria Sofia was waiting for us. We were wonderfully welcomed; Catarina's sister-in-law was kind and visibly glad about our return that her husband had wanted so much. The crowd threw their hats in the air, to our great delight. I remembered when we left, being a child, thirty years before. I remembered Alfonso's laughter of ill omen, his seizure, and his passing out. There was so much sadness then, matching the joy on that day of our return, when we came back exhausted from all we had endured.

We went together to the royal palace, where we learned that we already had a schedule, to which Catarina immediately agreed. I was allowed to spend a week in my brothers' house, and then I was supposed to go back and be at Catarina's disposal, so as to move. Until then, my house had already been prepared and arranged for us.

"Since you wrote to me that you would come back, beloved sister," said Pedro, "I have thought about having a palace built for you, where you could live, withdraw, and find your peace."

"I wanted to ask this of you," Catarina told him, taking his hand. "Juliana may live with her brothers for one week, if she promises that she will come and visit me every day. This is what I am accustomed to; this is the food I cannot be deprived of."

"I promise," I said to her, smiling.

Pedro continued, saying that he had made the decision that until the palace in Bemposta was ready for Catarina, we should live together in my house. They had made that decision together with my brothers, and I was quite pleased. The King said that he had bought some land in Bemposta, where there was just a chapel, which he would incorporate into the future palace, and that no one would bother us there.

In the meantime, Marisa was already at home, at my house, and she had started arranging the rooms, unpacking, and opening chests. She had seen my inheritance before I did. Marisa was met in the harbor by her brother and his wife, all crying with the joy of reunion. She had come home, too, after severely trying the nerves of the English captain of the ship. But we did not care about him; he would go back a few days later, taking with him everything that was connected to England. It was sunny and warm; birds were singing joyfully in the trees, and the windows were wide open, letting in the air full of lilac perfume.

After that meal, during which we talked excitedly, my brothers took me home, but not before assuring Catarina that I would come to see her every day until the house was ready, and that I would stay with her until the evening. The King thought it all well; we had to spend time with our families, to re-discover each other, to get to know our nephews, about whom I was very curious. Then we would settle in the house of the Countess of Alfambra, namely my mother, far from the noise and problems of the Court. There we could receive visitors, we could stay in the back yard, we could live unobserved. It was a very secluded house, and yet quite close to the center of Lisbon. I was most curious to see it myself, while Catarina did not know it at all.

I left, eager to see my relatives, but especially curious to see the children who were grown up now.

"Are you happy, my sister?" asked my elder brother in whose house I was supposed to live.

"Yes, it is only now that I feel I can truly breathe. I want to go and see the house my mother gave me; I haven't seen it for so long. I know you kept it up, and I thank you for that. I shall live with Catarina, but it is wonderful to have something of my own.

That week, I met and recognized so many people at the evening gatherings held by my brothers, whose houses were opposite one another. I met my nephews who stared at me as if I had come from another world. I was starting to get used to the warm weather, to the blue sky with no trace of rain.

Now two things persist in my mind, two things that touched me deeply: the visit to my parents' graves – actually the silence in the cemetery and the peace I found there, a kind of acceptance of the merciless fate – and the house I inherited from my mother. I stepped in and I remembered it right away: the wooden stairs that creaked from age, the clean kitchen like in the old times, two old servants whom I had left behind who had been in our service since then, the rooms upstairs, beautifully cared for with flowers at the windows, the street from where I could see every movement, the small parlor next to the bedroom… all that was wonderful and reminded me what it was like to live and to feel like living life to its fullest. Marisa showed me her room, too, smiling with delight.

Catarina's week at the royal palace was similar to mine, with many visitors, meeting her nephews, and getting to know the Queen better. Pedro held several tea parties in more restricted circles, which pleased Catarina, who felt re-welcomed in the bosom of her family. That same week, she also visited the graves of her family members, during which I accompanied her. She cried over the grave of that strange Alfonso; she knelt down at her mother's grave and seemed overwhelmed at the tomb of *Infanta* Isabela Louisa, Europe's beautiful fiancée, passed away so young, without knowing life.

"I shall be buried here as well, Juliana," she told me as we returned to the coach. I can barely wait to move. Sometimes I feel like a fifth wheel. The Queen is young, with children, one after the other, and I am fruitless."

"I was simply re-born," I answered, "when I saw my mother's house again. I am planning to make up for the past when I was unhappy, and that for as long as I live! I shall have happiness that has nothing to do with youth, but with my soul that is now starting to breathe."

"Maybe you are right in your own way; maybe you are stronger," she said, sighing. "Maybe you'll give me some of your strength."

"We are home. Nobody is yelling at us anymore because we are Catholics. We have God at last. Why don't we stop at that small church? No one will recognize us under these veils!"

"A very good idea," she said, letting her veil down over her eyes.

We went in. It was a lovely, peaceful church. There were only two monks inside, who were replacing the faded flowers with some fresh ones. We sat down and remained there, looking around us. Our eyes rested on the scenes from the Stations of the Cross, thinking that we had also made such a journey and that we had survived. Nobody bothered us while we were there, even though the monks stole a glance at us. We left with the fullness of God in our souls. When we reached the coach, we were comforted that we had gotten rid of pain and chagrin, that we had the liberty to pray to God as we considered fit. That was a powerful realization!

Catarina told me that Pedro knew from the monks about our life and all that we had suffered in England. At the same time, the Inquisition was underway in Portugal. It was also a kind of pursuit, a follow-up, only less serious, since we were obvious Catholics and eager to feel it freely and show that to the world. That same week, Catarina had a long discussion with her brother. My lady told her brother how much she would have liked to meet his first wife and child.

"But they are both gone now, and I am here to live on," she said sadly.

"I can only imagine what is in your heart, dear sister, but Maria Sofia is so good and kind that you will enjoy talking with her when you come over to the palace. But first I suppose you two need time to recover."

"Yes. Indeed, my greatest good fortune was and still is Juliana. She has always been there beside me, and I am blessed with her friendship. I was glad to learn that she would come and live with me when the Bemposta palace is ready. She has never regretted her fate tangled with mine, or the possibility to have remained in Portugal, to have married and had a happy life here."

"I know. Such devotion must be rewarded...."

"She had a great love, and she still carries this love in her heart. That was our cousin Gaspar, who was married to Antonia, dead five years after we arrived in England. I was a witness to their pure kiss, to their exchange of jewels as a memento, to their goodbye glances, all of that in my apartment. She is capable of great sacrifice, and to tell you the truth, she is still wearing on a golden chain the ring with the duke's inscription of the Medina Sidonia House which Gaspar gave her back then. I don't know whether Antonia noticed, but he gave away what was his most precious possession: his seal ring. When we embarked upon the ship to go to England, Gaspar sent her a letter and a lock of hair through a courier. I confess that the countess kept them next to Christ in her room."

"You will love the peace and quiet of Bemposta then. You will have things to meditate upon," Pedro said. "But first you will live at Juliana's, until that is all ready."

"One more thing, my beloved brother and King. I promised Juliana that I would take her to Spain to see her lover's grave. I think she deserves that. I kindly ask you to facilitate our journey there next year. She has the right to take some time and weep at the grave of the man she loved."

"Yes, I promise you I will take care of it all, for you to be able to leave in the spring, when it is not too hot," said Pedro, taking her sister's hands into his. "Are you content?"

"Yes, I am, with all my heart. I shall let my dear countess know about this gift from us."

I was overjoyed to learn about the King's decision. I remembered thanking Catarina with tears in my eyes, kissing her hands upon our meeting. Our departure to my house did not mean that we could not see our relatives or that they could not see us. It was just a secluded place, and we could leave that solitude only if we wanted to.

Around the same time, I recall being congratulated by the emissary of the Pope to our country for our strength in our parents' faith. I also thanked that mysterious character – at least that was my private opinion – assuring him of our desire to live in simplicity and prayer.

During that time, I came to know better Maria Sofia, the Queen. In my opinion, she was a wonderful woman who had done much for the country that had adopted her. The Portuguese loved her because she was a charitable person who helped poor people, widows, and orphans. She was also an open person, walking about the city and getting directly in touch with those people. She had also founded a school , the Franciscan School, which she led until her premature death. Her husband loved her and admired her for what she was doing, even if he afforded to make a slip sometimes. But Catarina did not appreciate those merits. She didn't understand the Queen's coming down among the people. She did not like her, and later on that animosity would increase. Maybe Catarina's antagonism was also because she was not allowed to be open toward her people in England. Maybe it was the trauma of the past reflecting upon her then. I never commented upon her opinion; I kept my thoughts to myself. I for one liked the palatine princess who became the Queen of Portugal and gave the country a heir who was then three years old.

My house was not a palace, but rather a villa, as Italians would call it, but it had all the necessary comforts in it. Upstairs, there were several rooms, impressive in their simplicity, and downstairs were the dining room, the parlor, a study, the kitchen, and the servants' rooms. There was enough room for five persons. When everything was set, Catarina loved it from the very beginning. It was so quiet! There were only the two of us upstairs, and the servants made very little noise anyway. Our rooms were facing the garden, so the sounds in the street did not reach us.

After we settled in, my brothers wanted to see us. Catarina received them willingly. We got used to that change quickly. We would attend Mass, and we would read in the garden. It was wonderful. Marisa helped us both get dressed and ready. She had been our maid for so many years. The old servant spent most of his time in the garden that he considered as his daughter, and his wife, also old, was in the kitchen most of the time.

After some time, we got used to our new status. I remember starting to write to Maria de Modena, James's wife, a bit afraid that she wouldn't be able to reply – who knew what situation she was in? My fear disappeared with the first letter I received from Maria. Waters were calmer then for them, and they were expecting a baby. That news truly pleased me, just like everything Maria wrote to me. She wrote beautifully, and it was a pleasure to read something written by her. I wrote back to her about our situation at that time, asking her to continue our correspondence which really brightened my existence. I was waiting for summer and for her to give birth to her child, so as to know that she and the baby were fine there in Saint-Germain-en-Laye. James was enjoying life, but he was troubled by his being so far away from his home and the injustice of his daughter. He enjoyed going for a walk, but there wasn't much else he could do, since he was just a helpless exile. He had been the King, but then he was no longer, and he had had to come to terms with that.

Catarina rejoiced over the news, and actually we began having a true correspondence, from which we learned quite a bit of the geography of the places where the former Queen and King were living with their little boy. I think that France is wonderful only by reading Maria's descriptions. As for the writing itself, I was the one doing that because Catarina was no longer interested in constantly having a correspondence. She was interested in all the news, she rejoiced, but she refused to write a couple of lines herself. She preferred praying, meditating on her life, and having long discussions that I also took part in, sometimes together with her personal priest. It seemed the climate change with constant sun tired her.

I just remembered something else. In my mother's house, we had only three servants. Catarina had declined any others from her brother. Sometimes we would go for a walk in the coach, and then, one day before, she would write to her brother for him to send us the crew, which Pedro was gladly doing.

Sometimes it was so quiet that it seemed my ears ached. Catarina had times when she wouldn't say a word for hours. She just stared blankly, and her eyes seemed to get troubled. She had become melancholic and she appreciated my not disturbing her. I would just stay there with a book in my hand, or at other times I would go out, unnoticed by the former Queen of England. I never asked her what she was seeing far away from the terrace where we were sitting.

Marisa would bring us news from time to time about Queen Maria Sofia, about how she was loved by the people, about how many charity acts she was doing for the poor people in town, and how she shook hands with them. Those manifestations gave her beautiful appearance a divine light, at least that was what the poor people said, and she was burning, in her turn, like a candle. To Pedro, she was a golden bridge between himself and the people. He admired and loved his wife even if he was unfaithful to her, having enough favorite ladies. But Maria seemed untroubled by that, for she had the children and her charity activity. She was always accompanied by two priests during her walks, and she was only 26 at that time.

Catarina was amazed and outraged, but she displayed her manifestations of disapproval only within our four walls, in a low voice and with me as sole witness.

95

At the end of summer, I received a letter from France. Maria had given birth to a girl in June, and she was feeling happier then as well as recovered. Louisa Maria Teresa, their little girl, was in good health, and James was a happy father. He was then busy with that darling little girl, and he had one more heir who made him forget his yearning for his country. Maria also told us that James no longer wanted the throne, but he would have liked to be able to kiss one more time the earth of his native country. That's man, kissing the hand of his executioner.

Coming back to the other Maria, Maria Sofia, she noticed her sister-in-law's coldness every time she met her. She knew that the former Queen of England did not like her, and in the public she too kept a cold silence and a calculated politeness. They just didn't like each other, that was all, and I did not interfere with that. What comes to my mind now occurred at a dinner that I attended when the Queen took me by the arm and told me smiling that she knew about Catarina's feelings for her, but that she did not mind at all.

"Catarina is someone for whom I feel sorry, considering everything she had to endure as a woman, and I pity her with all my heart. I feel no malice toward her. Difficulties in life made her irritable, and these dreary clothes keep her far from the world, for she just closes up inside herself," the Queen said.

I didn't reply to those words. I just said that no one would find out from me what Maria Sofia confessed in private by the window. I made a gesture of majestic reverence and left under the gaze of that young lady. I don't think Catarina noticed our short discussion, for she was talking to a cardinal in a more private place. I never told her that the Queen understood her so well, and she never had any proof of my discussion with Maria Sofia, either. The subject was closed, and it has never been resumed between me and the sovereign.

This is in essence how the first year in Portugal passed, after waiting so long to return to our native land: adjusting, sometimes going to the palace, praying in the church nearby as I waited for spring to come so that we could leave for Spain. I knew that Pedro was taking care of everything through his secretaries. We spent New Year's Eve praying and studying the layout of the Bemposta palace. The chapel was indeed the center from which the palace was being built surrounding it. Catarina was thrilled. I was dreaming about Spain, while she was dreaming about her future palace at Bemposta.

CHAPTER 14

As a gift from Catarina, I received that letter in which she was informed of her cousin Gaspar's death in 1667. I put it next to the cross in my room. It was yellowed with age, but anything related to her cousin was precious to me. I was amazed by my friend's capacity to keep that news to herself for so long, and then the fact that she gave me that letter that very year, 1693, when I wanted to go on a pilgrimage to his grave. He had died young at 37. Because his wife Antonia had not given him any children, the title of Duke was awarded to his stepbrother, after his mother, Anna Maria de Guzman.

That 11th Duke of Medina Sidonia was alive and he was informed of our arrival. Pedro received a reply in which the Duke Juan Claros wrote that he was expecting us with joy and curiosity at the same time; he was especially waiting to see the former Queen of England. He was honored, as was his wife Mariana. She was actually his second wife. His first wife, Antonia Teresa Pimentel, had passed away some time ago, but she had given him the heir to the Duke's title. Manuel Perez de Guzman y Pimentel, the duke-to-be, was 22 in 1693. He was in his prime of life, looking exactly like his mother, as we would see later on.

Let's come back to my lover. Everybody was making considerable efforts for me to be able to visit his grave. Gaspar Juan was the son of Gaspar Alfonso Perez, the 9th Duke of Medina Sidonia, conceived with his first wife Anna Maria de Guzman. He had had brothers, too, but they all died; he was the only one who survived. He was born in 1630, and when I met him, he was 32 and he was not yet a duke. His father lived two more years. His marriage to Antonia was one of convenience; Antonia was the daughter of Luis Mendez de Haro, the 6th Marquis of Carpio, and she was a jealous, sterile, and stingy woman. Their marriage was a failure; the two of them did not love each other, especially after Antonia realized that she

97

could not have children, which led to a sick jealousy. I didn't know much about him. I was looking forward to that trip to clarify some things for me, too, to see a portrait, or something remaining from him. But there was still time left until March. Everything was ready. We needed only the right weather to leave, for we were going to sail into the harbor of Cadiz and from there we would go to the city of Medina Sidonia in one of the Duke coaches prepared for that purpose.

So these lines are about me, at an age when I should normally have had children and grandchildren. But here I was, reliving my chaste youth with all its related dreams. I knew that the King of Portugal had arranged everything and I was both eager and nervous at the same time. It felt as if I were going to see Gaspar Juan himself, and not just to visit his grave. My heart was beating rapidly, just as it had back then in Catarina's apartment. When I looked at the lock of hair and the Duke's ring, melancholy would seize me. I had also the two letters. Those were my treasures. I was grateful to Catarina for joining me on that trip, thus helping me to see my dream come true. She just smiled at me, saying that was the least she could do for me to reward me for my devotion.

"And then, Juliana, I'm also curious to see my mother's relatives, so I am a kind of ambassador on this journey. You've come with me everywhere I've gone, and I shall do the same for you. We shall never be apart," Catarina told me, arranging her sleeve laces.

I thanked my friend with tears in my eyes, telling her I truly hoped I would meet Gaspar Juan in heaven, and I confessed to her that I had prayed to God to take me to Him sooner, thus fulfilling my dream. Catarina embraced me and told me, as if she were talking to a child, that I should not think of something like that.

"You will go to heaven when the right time comes; do not offend God," Catarina went on.

Certainly, it seemed that I still had many years to live and that I wouldn't see heaven opening up for me too soon. I felt good, nothing troubled me, and the closer the journey, the better I felt, as if I had been growing younger, becoming livelier and stronger.

I had decided to take with me a pot with an ivy, and leave it there for my beloved one. I was going to plant it, and the ivy would spread everywhere for always. Catarina thought my idea was not bad. On the same occasion, regarding the ivy, she told me that Juan Claros knew the purpose of that trip, and he was glad that there had been someone who had loved his brother, that he didn't die without knowing what love is – which he discovered quite by accident. I was surprised by that news, but my friend reassured me, feeling that he was a good-hearted brother. She also told me that Pedro had been corresponding with him, and he had described me and told about our short history.

"Who knows what pleasant surprises are waiting for you in Spain?" she said afterwards, getting up from her armchair and going out onto the terrace.

What I learned then touched me deeply, but I decided to leave myself in the hands of Fate. I wasn't interested in the relations between Spain and Portugal, which had become open with the reign of Catarina's father; I knew there was a certain animosity between the two countries, or better said, their relations were strained, with an icy politeness holding many implications.

The King's officials had given us all the necessary papers and approvals for our visit. I was just Catarina's chaperone. The reason for *Infanta*'s visit was to see her mother's relatives and their graves, if they had died. And indeed that was the case. It was a plausible and genuine motive. Thus, we easily obtained the approvals from the Spanish.

When March came, the ship was ready for departure. We were supposed to travel only along the coast of Spain, thus reaching Cadiz. The captain had decided to make two stops, for supplies in the harbor of Lagos, and on the Spanish side, in Huelva, before arriving in Cadiz. We decided to send letters to Lisbon and Medina Sidonia from these two harbors, thus informing them about all the events that occurred on our way. Marisa did not come with us, for her legs ached terribly, so we had only the servants brought by the King at our service.

My brothers were glad that I would see my dream come true, and they wished me a safe trip and a speedy return to them. I was eager to reach our destination. The weather was lovely, just as the King said. We had a full court with us; the House of Braganza had to show its independence somehow, and that was a good opportunity to do so.

It was the end of March, one year after our return from England, where nothing significant had changed during that year. The Duke of Gloucester, William, was living even with his deformed head, and strange as he was. But thinking about Alfonso, nothing seemed strange anymore. *Infanta* was feeling good. Apparently she had come out of her lethargy that sometimes took long and tiring hours for me. She remembered how she had said goodbye to the Queen before leaving. Maria Sofia had been accompanied by the two boys, Joao, who was four, and Francisco, who was only one. She confessed to me that she had been a bit jealous of that wonderful mother and her children.

We did not stay long in Lagos, stopping there for the supplies. The weather continued to be gorgeous, and the captain wanted to take advantage of it. I don't even know when we entered the territorial waters of Spain. We could see the shore quite near, with the dry red soil, and we could see the people stopping to watch the ship of the Braganza House. Some of them herded the flocks of sheep on those dry hills while others had different occupations which we could not see too well through the spyglass, for the ship was moving quickly.

In Huelva, we had letters waiting from us from Portugal as well as from Spain. We did not want to disembark, for our own safety. That was the captain's advice, and we strictly obeyed it. We read the letters secure in my cabin. We did not go out on the deck except for a short time in the evening.

In Spain, Carlos II was ruling – the irony! – he had the same name (in Spanish) as Catarina's husband; an unfortunate man with no children, and very ill; he had written his will when he was young, thereby ending the continuity of the Habsburg House in favor of the French House of Bourbon. The poor man was like Alfonso, seeing day after day his direction toward his own coffin. But let us not talk about sad things.

We were to be met in Cadiz by the Duke of Medina Sidonia himself, namely Juan Claros. The Duchess was not with him, but the Duke had quite an entourage. He greeted Catarina with great joy. He kissed his aunt's hand and cordially greeted me as well. Then the servants started carrying the chests to the coach. Until we reached the town he was ruling, we travelled in the same roomy coach that had the Duke's coat of arms on both sides, an insignia I found odd because of the serpents in baskets in the center. We soon left Cadiz, the largest harbor of Spain, traveling on countryside roads where the red dust mercilessly rose up, making me sneeze. The Duke assured me that our destination was not far away and that in a short while we would have all the necessary comforts at our disposal.

Indeed, he was right about that; we could see the town and the Duke's palace from behind a hill, rather a red stone hillock. Duchess Mariana greeted us, smiling, and immediately showed us the rooms where we would rest. The palace was beautiful, built of white stone, which contrasted sharply with the red color of the soil. Behind it was an olive orchard, like a real forest, probably covering a shaded park. The window of my room overlooked that side of the building. Catarina had a window in front where she could see a fountain from which water was sprang in a wide circle with stone fish on the edge. It was really beautiful; it made me forget how dry everything was around it. And yet, I think I was most

100

fortunate; I loved that olive grove with its row of benches made from the same stone as the building.

Taking a closer look around my room, I noticed on the table a jewel, and I thought about letting the duchess know about it when I looked again, and then rushed over to it. It was the medallion that Gaspar Juan wore at his neck, the one I had given him. I took my lock of hair out. What a surprise! I knelt down and burst out crying. I put the lock of hair back and fastened the medallion at my neck. I was again its owner. I went to Catarina, who understood what I had found by simply looking at my neck and recognizing the jewel.

"Juliana, my dear, Antonia has never known about this jewel. The current duke took it from his brother's hands when he no longer had the strength to speak before he died. He loved you as much as you loved him, and Juan Claros wanted to surprise you and try you at the same time. Well, you passed his test; you recognized the jewel. Tomorrow, we'll go to see the graves of the fearless dukes that I come from, and you will be planting that ivy. Now, if you are ready, and more relaxed, let's go downstairs. They are waiting for us."

"She passed the test, nephew," Catarina said, while going downstairs. "She has the medallion at her neck, as you can see."

"I am so glad, countess," the duke said, smiling. "His last words were for you, and heard only by me. He loved you, and he said that he would wait for you in heaven; there, maybe God will do justice and you will be together."

"Thank you," I said, scarcely containing my tears, when I felt someone's arm around my waist. It was Mariana, the Duchess, who smiled at me, reassuring me and seeing me to the place where the table was laid.

During the meal, we spoke about the family torn apart, one branch in Portugal and another in Spain. It was a quiet meal, where one could feel the calm and understanding between the two spouses. Mariana didn't have children either, but Juan Claros had a heir from his first wife, Antonia Teresa Pimentel, who had passed away years ago. I've mentioned this young man before; at the time, he was in Castilia, on business with some old relatives of theirs.

After the meal, we entered a small salon situated right next to the dining room. We made ourselves comfortable in armchairs, to have tea, and the duke rang the bell. Immediately, two servants came in with sleeves rolled up and carrying in their hands something large and rectangular, wrapped in canvas. Mariana led me by the hand before a painting. I removed the canvas, and I gasped, then burst out crying. It was a portrait of my dear Gaspar Juan. It was so true-to-life, so veridical. It was so like his face as I remembered it from back then in Catarina's room.

"Dear countess, when my brother came home, he decided to have his portrait made, an idea that he had rejected until then. He told me that he had lost his ring, and that made me curious for the second time. Gaspar was so serious, so meticulous, and never forgot anything, but I said nothing. He immediately ordered another ring made, which I'm wearing right now," the Duke said to me, holding out his hand to me and showing me the ring.

"I have his ring," I said, revealing it at my neck.

"And it shall remain there," Mariana said, smiling.

"And the painting is all yours," Catarina laughed, clapping her hands. I took it then.

"Dear aunt, you are indeed an intuitive nature. The painting belongs without a doubt to the countess," the Duke said. "On his dying bed, my brother ordered me that if I ever found the Countess of Alfambra, I should give this to her. I want to emphasize that until then, he had refused to have his portrait painted next to Antonia. You will get to see her; she is depicted alone in a painting, with the same pale face, but – please forgive me – but as they say, speak no evil of the dead."

I confess I had fallen asleep late, and the candle lit my room for a long time. I was looking at the painting that I would take home with me. In the space left by Gaspar's portrait, they had hung a painting with my beloved one as a child, next to his mature wife, which seemed a bit unnatural, but the family gallery had to be complete. I had embraced the painting so many times, and I was already dreaming about the place where I would put it in my home. It will of course be hung in my bedroom, safe from the public eye. He had been faithful to me, and I had been faithful to him. We were united forever before God. I had had so many surprises only in a couple of hours since we arrived in Spain. Late that night, after midnight, I put out the candle and fell asleep, my heart at ease. We were to spend two more weeks there, and then we would return to Portugal.

I will pass over the unimportant details of our trip. The next day, Catarina, the Duchess, and I went to the burial chamber belonging to the family of the dukes of Medina Sidonia. They were all buried there next to their wives. The old marble of my dear Gaspar Juan was partially green. His name, birth year, and death year were written on the plaque. Antonia's place was next to his; she had died after him, as I'd learned. There were so many inscriptions everywhere, it was like a museum, but my impression was that everything was too cold and I couldn't find my duke there. I told

102

that to Catarina, who understood, whispering to me that he was in my heart, and in my heart only. I came out of there and decided to plant the ivy next to the door. I hoped that it would spread and cling to the entire building. Mariana had promised me that she would take care to train it on a wire so that it could reach the roof. After planting it, I prayed that it would take root, and then we started walking in the cemetery. Catarina had brought flowers, which she laid on the cold marble of her grandparents, and made a connection in her mind between Luiza, her mother, and Louiza's parents who were also far, far away from their daughter.

I visited the graves every day. They were not far from the Duke's palace, and I knew the road by myself. Toward the end of the two weeks, I felt certain that my ivy had grown roots into the ground of Spain. Mariana ordered the caretaker to get some nails and string a wire onto which the ivy could cling; she also ordered him to water it every day and take good care of it. I gave him some money for that job, but he replied to me:

"I would do anything for Doña Mariana! I don't need money! She is so kind to my family. The other duchess who slept in there had never looked at me. Her husband paid me for my work and helped me every now and then, but she was so proud, so arrogant, and I was so unimportant that she didn't have time for such an insignificant mortal like me. She closed her eyes sooner than I – and that also with my help. I forgave her a long time ago."

What struck me was the openness with which he spoke about Duchess Antonia; to him she was just an ordinary woman who died like ordinary people and lived very much the same way, whom he had buried and was then taking care of. He also told me that he prayed for the Virgin Mary to forgive her for her unkindness.

On our last evening, I also met the heir to the title of Duke. That young man, a bit over 20, looked something like his father, but his cheeks were far more delicate. He probably looked like Antonia Pimentel, his mother, whose painting I had also noticed in the gallery.

Everything was set for our departure. All the gifts we had received were already on the ship, and the ship was loaded with supplies. I had grown younger during that visit, and our way back seemed shorter, maybe also because we did not stop in Huelva, but only in Lagos, from where I wrote letters to the Duke, the King, and my brothers. On the ship, I told Catarina that I felt at peace and that I was waiting to set foot on the soil of my country.

When we arrived, everybody noticed how much good the trip had done us, for we were all fresh. The whole family was pleased with what

103

they saw. It was around late April, or even early May. The weather was lovely, even if a bit hot. I had re-arranged my room, hanging the painting on the wall. I was so happy to have Gaspar was looking at me every time I looked at the canvas – only he was young, and I was old. I was amused by that.

We received a letter from Spain, in which Mariana let me know that the ivy was growing strong, and that they had put next to its roots, on the lower edge of the building, a plaque on which they had written my name and the fact that the ivy was a gift from me to the duke who had passed away in 1667. I do want to emphasize that this gesture impressed me for eternity, for everybody will know about me now. It was interesting. I wrote her back, thanking her, and at the same time, I sent a letter to France, in which I described to Maria our trip to Spain.

We spent the rest of our time just as we had in England, going for walks around Lisbon, where nobody even suspected who we were, and where we had no fear to walk. Of course, we were always accompanied by a few servants. Marisa would have joined us, but her legs were too weak. Her brother came to see her quite frequently, for she couldn't go out much anymore. Sometimes she would go to the garden, but that was about all that she could do. The dampness in England had affected her bones, weakening them.

Maria Sofia, Portugal's Queen, was pregnant and was about to give birth the following year. That would have been the fourth child of the Queen, and the sixth of the King, considering *Infanta* Isabela from the first marriage, and her natural, acknowledged daughter, Luisa de Braganza, who was only fourteen in 1693. Maria Sofia was not upset by those mistresses and their children. She loved her husband, and her calmness and kindness always brought him back to her. Those women were just passing, just temporary, while she was his wife, the one who had given him the heir. Thus, the year 1693 passed as well, and it was full but at the same time enjoyable for us.

CHAPTER 15

We enjoyed one more winter like those of our childhood, without powerful winds, without continuously burning the fire in the fireplace. One day we even went on the shore of the Atlantic and gathered shells, just as we used to do when we were children. We put them by the windows of the living room, where we spent almost our entire day. We took pleasure in reading the letters received from Maria, telling us about the amusing pranks of her two children, about their teeth that were coming in or coming out, depending on the age of each child. Maria was amused, and that amused us, too. Catarina was listening, but not paying attention. Just the same, I had to let her know about any piece of news I heard, even if she didn't have much to say about it.

That year, 1694, Maria Sofia gave birth to a little girl who brought joy to the family for a short while. *Infanta* Francisca Xaviera died immediately after her birth, to everyone's sorrow. Pedro was inconsolable, for he had wanted that little girl so much, in memory of his first child. Crying and mourning seized us all at the funeral of that small girl. I thanked God, though, that the little girl had been baptized and thus was at rest with Him, entering His Kingdom as an angel. Only her father, who had wanted her so much, was more difficult to console, for he was only father then, and not the King.

I wrote to Maria about that sad story, and Maria sympathized with us from a distance. We were surprised by the note from Louise, which Maria included with her letter. Louise told us how she had been dispossessed of the gifts she received from Charles II, how her pension had been taken right after 1688, how she was living in Paris on the mercy of King Louis XIV, but handled it well. Catarina just shrugged her shoulders and said:

"And what would have this woman expected? That Mary II should double her pension? Do you remember what we went through and how constrained we lived? How could Mary have paid her uncle's mistress? I think that Louise, as she grows older, no longer has the liveliness we once loved so much. Neither do lovers wait in a queue at her door, nor can she be a spy anymore. She is 45 years old, and her life as a *femme fatale* is all gone now. Sometimes I am glad I have not been beautiful; maybe I would have been drawn to coquetry and who knows what I would be doing right now. Excess is always destructive. I am just glad she is in good health and that France's King is giving her a pension, but that is not living; that is like a prison, considering the kind of youth full of excess that she had. Now it is hard for her, and I understand her, but what can I do for her from here? Nothing."

I let her talk. Catarina had forgotten that Louise did not ask for her help, but was simply telling us about herself, just as old friends do. Her star had come down as well, eventually, just as the stars of all the old and penniless courtesans. I recalled Barbara then, but only for a second. We all grow old, and unless we have the intelligence to live while accepting it, life becomes a burden, an iron ball tied to one's leg as with prisoners. Old age has its own charm if the spirit stays awake and young. Catarina felt her age, but I didn't. When I look at that dear painting in my room, I am still the one who stole the heart of her beloved, at that time young and handsome.

There was some restlessness at the Court, with Maria Sofia being pregnant again. Catarina was a bit worried:

"These frequent pregnancies will kill her, but if God makes her have babies, then she will have to bear her cross."

I had the same opinion. She had just lost her baby and was expecting again in 1695. The Queen hoped that the baby would also be a little girl.

I eventually wrote back to Louise at the address in Paris that she indicated in her note. I didn't write her much, just the essentials of our lives. Catarina's attitude made me write to her that way; consequently, I knew I would not receive an answer from her too soon.

I received instead news from somewhere else, that time via our diplomatic channel. Mary II of England had died from smallpox at only 32. Her father had been told about it, but he was not allowed to set foot on the soil of his country, which was why he remained in France without saying goodbye to his daughter who defied and humiliated him so much. I sent him a condolence letter to France, to which he replied, thanking us.

106

William III of Orange reigned all alone, yearning for his wife and remaining disconsolate. He refused to get married again and implicitly, to have any more children with someone else, children who could have carried on his name. Everybody was looking at the Duke of Gloucester, who at that time was five and still alive, even if with physical disabilities.

Of course, we did not attend the funeral; we were merely represented by the Ambassador. The Royal House had also sent an official condolence letter, to which Catarina added a few personal lines in memory of her niece. But as with everything in this world, it all passes; everything is transformed and then vanishes.

In 1695, Maria Sofia gave birth to another child, that time a little boy, who did survive. He was baptized Antonio. The Queen regained self-confidence as the days passed, and the baby was alive and kicking, as they say. At the christening party, Pedro was joyful and had so much fun, even though he did not have any girls, if we do not take into account Luiza , her mother Maria da Cruz Mascaren having long been forgotten. After Antonio's birth, Maria Sofia seemed to change a little to those who knew her better. She displayed the same calmness in front of everybody, the same kindness, and the same willingness, but sometimes a cloud would darken her forehead, but went away immediately. It was as if her soul didn't burn for her anymore as it used to before then, but only for others, to a great extent. Was she bothered by her husband's unhappiness because of his desire to have a little girl? What kind of sacrifice was this Queen trying to make? But I was the only one from our circle who noticed. I did not have anyone to talk to on that subject, for I knew that the Queen would do her best for Pedro to have a girl. And yes, the following year, she did give birth to a little girl, a lovely little girl, whom they called Teresa Maria.

So many children, we thought! So much hustle and bustle! So many christenings and parties! All those little plump pink legs! I insist upon mentioning that I was really thrilled about that. I had preserved the spontaneity of youth, which I cannot say about Catarina, who was more and more impervious and did not have a close relationship with the Queen, who wasn't upset though. I must confess that Maria Sofia had recovered with a bit more difficulty after that birth. She spent two more weeks in bed, compared to her previous pregnancies.

Catarina was like a baby who had found her favorite toy. She was taking care of her future palace at Bemposta, which was slowly being built; we were far from moving into it any time soon. My friend took care of the layout. She had long discussions with the architect, and she wanted to have the coat of arms on the front side, for it to be as visible as possible, plus many other small things and details of the kind.

After she recovered, the Queen continued her charity work as well as her children's education. Soon, she would learn that she was pregnant again. She was like a martyr to us. She was truly glad when the doctor confirmed that new pregnancy. In fact, she was still young; she was 30. This is when Infant Manuel, Earl of Ourem, was born. The Queen recovered quickly, and when she appeared in public, she looked quite well; I noticed that even the clouds on her forehead were disappearing, lightening her spirit. Those clouds, we were to find out, were caused by her husband, who had a new mistress – or better said, a new favorite. If she did not get to know his first favorite, well, she did know that second one; it was Anne Armands de Verger. I could see that the Queen was hurt, while striving to preserve her dignity, and the clouds were still there. Catarina noticed that, too, and one day she told me, outraged:

"I cannot understand how my brother shares two beds: the Queen's, whom he afflicted with those births, who closes her eyes against her pain and screams alone – and this favorite's bed, whom I despise! If only she had been spiritual like Louise. Maybe for a time, the Queen will not give birth anymore. At least he should let her recover. Let that favorite have babies!"

I made no comment. I remember that I worked and pretended to be extremely busy with my embroidery frame. Catarina was talking and disregarded my agitation on that topic, which I had lived through before in England. My friend had forgotten her own pain, the pain she had felt, and was revolting against some other woman's pain.

So the next year, no baby was born in the royal family; apparently, the King had gone more to his mistress's bed. But in 1698, something terrible for our faith happened. Both the Queen and the favorite were pregnant. That pregnancy of the Queen was painful to her. She would not speak to us, and her smile was gone completely; she would put on a smile only when absolutely mandatory, but even then it was distorted. The King did not notice his wife's sorrow. The unhappiness and the affliction of carrying that pregnancy made the whole Court whisper. We could not talk about that topic with the Queen, and our visits to the royal palace seemed too long.

When the time came, the Queen gave birth to a little girl, in late January of 1699, and then the favorite gave birth to a child whom the King acknowledged and whom they baptized Miguel. Unfortunately, Maria Sofia did not recover entirely. She managed to get out of bed, to grit her

108

teeth and fulfill her role, but she would never say what pain she was in, until her compassionate smile was gone completely, and it became impossible for her to go out in the street anymore to her people.

Those pregnancies tired her terribly, and the pain she felt was obvious. She could no longer hide it. Doctors had recommended that she get some rest and take a trip far from Lisbon's social whirl, maybe also to be away from that favorite and her child. No one could say, of course. Always compliant, the Queen accepted the doctor's recommendation and left on that recovery retreat, which the King whole-heartedly approved, first because he needed Maria Sofia for the bridge she represented between him and the people, and second, because he wanted to spend some time at ease with his mistress.

But when she came back, the Queen looked much worse. She had deep dark rings around her eyes, and she was pale and thinner. On her welcome visit, she told Catarina that she had written a kind of memoir which she wanted Catarina to keep and give to her husband at some point in time. She did not say "at her death"; I think she still hoped to live.

The doctor had a talk with the King, who was unhappy with his wife's weakness. The diagnosis was withheld, and the doctor suggested, in so many words, that the inevitable would happen sooner or later, depending on God's will. The Queen was only 32, but her pregnancies had weakened her considerably.

"And not only have you lost weight, Your Majesty, but your heart beats irregularly, the lungs sound different, you've lost your appetite, and your stomach is affected," the doctor detailed it.

"But I don't want to lose her," Pedro said to himself, but in a loud voice when he was left alone in his study.

Eventually, the Queen came to understand the inevitable that the entire court was hiding from her. The favorite had been banished to afford more tranquility. Even the common people, with their feeble minds, understood the news of their beloved Queen's disease. Because of her weakened condition, the Queen also became ill with erysipelas, her face swelling and becoming more deformed every day. Maria Sofia resigned herself and told that to her husband. She kissed her children with passion as if it would be the last time, and they were shocked by their mother's transformation. They thanked heaven for every day she received. Pedro became dispirited. It was a very sad situation.

The people kept watch in front of the palace doors, waiting for some good – or bad – news, as well as to see the Queen at the balcony. The Queen was becoming more disfigured every day. The mirrors had been covered, and the servants were no longer allowed to be astonished by anything. Maria Sofia wasn't getting up from her bed anymore, and Pedro was about to become a widower for the second time. He had solemnly promised his wife he would not get married again.

When the Queen felt that her end was drawing near, she received Communion, and asked to see her children and us as well, being called to come quickly. She said goodbye, in peace, kissing her children with no tears. Once she took Communion, she became calm. She said goodbye to Pedro, forgiving him from her heart. She died like a saint on the 4th of August, 1699, two days before turning 33. She was lamented like a martyr, and the people were allowed near her coffin. The Portuguese mourned that hand that would no longer caress them, and they buried her with peace full of grief.

Pedro seemed destroyed. We always realize what we lose after we can no longer do anything about it. It was his fault, he said to himself, too many pregnancies and too many mistresses. Catarina gave him the journal of Maria Sofia, the one she had written on her last trip, which hadn't improved her health. After reading it, Pedro sank into deep sadness, from which only wars would lift him. He had designated Catarina Regent during his absence. Joao was still underage. Catarina accepted that mission, too.

The death of his wife opened the door to many other deaths, which we, the living, had to accept and subsequently turned our thoughts inward. During the next years, Pedro lived peacefully, trying to recover after the great loss of his wife; the Lord had called many to Him, to our bewilderment.

The Duke of Gloucester, the Stuarts' hope, let his guard down and passed away, tired of the life he had had. He was born the same year as Joao, and his death frightened Pedro. Anyone may die, just as William, Anne's only child, died. The century had begun badly for the Stuart house. We again sent a condolence letter, to which Anne replied, overwhelmed with grief. They were all going, and indeed one could see the House of Hanover on the horizon, waving its colors. She was just helpless, and she couldn't have any more children after so many miscarriages. I did not reply to her after that. What else could we have said to her? Nothing could comfort her anymore; she had to find the necessary strength within herself.

The next year, it was Maria of Modena's turn to weep for her husband. James passed away sad, far from his country, being buried there in Saint-Germain-en Laye, mourned by his wife and his two children who were there next to him. What would have happened if his son, a catholic Stuart, had gone on to become King? But that was an impossible story. No one would have accepted a Catholic on the England's throne. They would rather have accepted another Royal House than legitimate Catholics.

Continuing chronologically, the year after we moved in to the beautiful Bemposta Palace, England's Protestant King passed away. After many escapades that William had while riding a horse, he fell off the horse and was badly injured. He recovered, but succumbed to pneumonia because of the excessive dampness of those lands. He did not have any heirs, so the next in line to the throne was Anne, the last Stuart on the throne. The peaceful Queen rejoiced in the love of her husband, the Prince Consort George, although they had no heirs. They lived also in Kensington Palace, and they preferred the moderate party to rule the country, namely the "Tories," who were less intransigent.

I have previously mentioned that in 1702 we moved to Bemposta, but before that event anticipated ever since we returned from England, we lived for a while in the royal palace. Catarina was designated Regent for Joao. In 1701, Pedro had the strength to leave for war, for the succession to the Spanish throne. That young man, Carlos II, sick but still alive thanks to his strong spirit, had passed away in November of 1700. Philip V succeeded him to the throne, written in his will upon the deathbed of the late King. Thus, for the Habsburg House, Carlos's death meant losing Spain's throne in favor of the French, namely the Bourbon House. It was essentially the same story as in England, where the Stuart House was losing the throne in favor of the Hanover House.

A period with so many twisted events and so many deaths made us witnesses to important changes in the destiny of some of the great powers of that time. When Pedro came back, we withdrew with relief to Catarina's palace. We had taken Marisa with us, leaving only a few servants in my house, just to take care of it.

Bemposta was a lovely palace, having Catarina's coat of arms engraved upon the main entrance. The chapel in the middle was interesting. Its incorporation into the palace was a good idea. One could not possibly get lost, because you would have inevitably come upon the chapel. Catarina spent a lot of time there, for it was so quiet and there were so few people living there. What an ugly century we were given to live in. Only Louis XIV amazed us, for he was still young and strong, burying all the Kings of his generation. He was born in 1638, just like Catarina, but you should have seen the force, the vigour he displayed! He was a feared King in Europe, especially since he had a tyrannical position toward the Protestants.

Pedro had been right to have the Bemposta Palace built; we settled down in that palace, and we appeased our hearts' turmoil at last. The

111

palace had a charming park, with lovely trees and benches we could sit on together whenever we were separately feeling lonely. We listened to the rustle of trees, and we looked at the flowers in the palace garden, thus forgetting everything else. A great sadness was the fact that Marisa could no longer walk. Servants would carry her on their backs and let her down in an armchair specially prepared for her. A young servant stayed with her permanently, reading to her from the Bible. She would rarely speak, and she often stared blankly, listening to the young woman's voice. She was then being served, for she could no longer serve others.

One day, we learned that Marisa had requested that a priest come and give her Communion. In the past few days, she had spoken very little, and she had eaten little. She would answer our questions only by looking at us. She passed away the next morning. When Catarina learned of Marisa's death, she exclaimed, "Everybody is leaving us, everybody is dying!" Crying bitter tears, we buried her in the park at the root of a lovely tree. She had been irreplaceable to us all our lives, and now she would remain just a shadow, a cherished memory.

That was an ugly period. Marisa was not immortal, either; there was our humid English past in her bones. The Lord had taken her to Himself, making her happy. We were now the only ones left alive, like two rocks next to the sea, which regardless of how battered they would have been, they remained stalwart, not falling into the waves. God still wanted us alive, maybe because He still had tasks for us. The cold stone was not yet for us.

CHAPTER 16

Now I hope that I haven't bored those who have read the last few pages, causing them not to continue this passage. I feel that I had to write that tedious reminder of these sad events, this chain of deaths. There were many, indeed, and some of them had great significance, as for instance, the death of the unfortunate William, with whom so many hopes were related and whom I knew personally. I will say again, that was an ugly beginning to the new century.

After the sad events in France, I continued my correspondence with Maria de Modena. I tried to comfort her, reminding her that she had the children, she had something to live for, but honestly I think we were also just tired. We were weary with life, with so much fighting and suspense. The heir of the throne was fourteen then, and that year, 1703, he promised to turn into a handsome young man, besides the fact that he was intelligent. He came to visit about once a week, when he was finished with all his teachers who were teaching him the rules and procedures related to his future role as King. I think he realized that they were necessary, but they bored him considerably. After his mother's death, he had grown very deeply attached to his Aunt Catarina, and she grew fond of him, too. Thus, she could influence him in many respects, as she wished. We liked his youth and his hope of doing something good, his enthusiasm, the awareness that one day he would rule the country, that he would be the King, replacing his father. He asked his aunt to tell him memories from the Court of England, and Catarina always found amusing stories to tell him, which stimulated his young mind. Those tales influenced strongly the desire to do only what was his duty for the future, but he was still just a child. Fourteen years old is still quite young, I am thinking – with my old, but still active mind.

He was the best heir for Pedro, and I got the chance to know him when he was innocent and with no vice, of which he was guilty later on. We prayed only that the King would stay alive, for he was quite ill at that time.

We occasionally received letters from Paris, from Louise, who told us that she was ruined and unhappy in her privation. When I told that to Catarina, she would just wave her hand in boredom. Only that child who was about to become King would spark her to life. One day, I remember it very well, we visited the Jeronimos monastery, and Catarina's eyes lit up when she saw her brother Alfonso's gravestone.

"I shall lie there soon," she said.

I tried to tell her not to think that way, but she made the same sign with her hand, which had become usual, and so I kept silent. After all, she knew better. That year, Pedro became the father of another child, a little boy whom he acknowledged and called Jose. His son's mother was the beautiful Francisca Clara da Silva, and he was the fruit of 1702. Jose was the last of Pedro's children. Pedro had grown too tired, even though he was ten years younger than Catarina.

The next year, though, he was bedridden because of a serious disease, from which he barely recovered in 1705. What could have been the reason? Possibly the death of *Infanta* Teresa Maria, who was only seven. Pedro had adored his daughters all his life. He thought that boys should be brought up strictly, in the military style, but girls should be raised in exactly the opposite way – they should be spoiled and adored. Poor man saw many of his daughters perish during his life, not to mention the overwhelming disappointment caused by the death of Princess of Beira, *Infanta* from his first marriage.

"All my girls are dying!" he shouted, raving and biting his bed sheet. "I have only one daughter left, Francisca Josefa. You want to take her, too, to You, God? What do you need her for? Can't you take someone else?"

All the people at the palace believed he was going to die, so during that period, Catarina became Queen Regent again for her beloved Joao. That turn of events made us leave Bemposta Palace again, and we didn't know when we would come back. The people of the court viewed Joao as the future King. The boy had long discussions with his aunt, who told him many interesting and useful things, some related to England, others related to the governing of a country. Joao was very attentive; he loved his father's sister.

114

The Regent gave orders that people should pray in every church in the larger cities of the country, for the good health of the King, and those prayers were heard, to our relief. Pedro fought hard, but he recovered from the ailment that had seized him for so long. He was able to resume his duties as a King. We were glad when, in the summer of 1705, we could return to Bemposta in peace.

On one of the warm evenings of that season, Catarina called me into the garden. She calmly told me that she had had a dream in which someone was throwing her off a precipice, but when she tried to get up, she didn't have the strength. Nobody answered her, and both she and her horse had fallen. She was young and beautiful, and the events of the dream brought with them the flavor of England. That precipice was for certain there in England.

"I shall die, Juliana, I can feel it. Look, I want you to open this letter once I am gone."

I took the letter and could not say anything, for Catarina had already made me that sign that meant *Say nothing more*, the usual sign. I left her in her silence, and I plunged into my own.

"Read it in the presence of my brother and my dear nephew, " she said eventually.

I know that after the visit in 1703, at the Jeronimos monastery, she had arranged her last resting place, but I did not attach any importance to that. It was just a momentary fear or impulse, in my opinion. But in fact, if I had thought about it, it was neither of those. We were both quite old. She would turn 67 in November. She had reason to be concerned. Only I had the same lively spirit, maybe in part because I had not been married, and I had not had those difficulties come directly upon me. The King did not know about those things; since he had been so sick for so long, no one troubled him with insignificant details.

After that dream, she almost never came out of her room, and whenever I would come into her room, she barely spoke. I don't think I was unwelcome – I had never been. I just believe she was thinking about other things that were truly important. Maybe deep down in her heart, she was saying goodbye to life, struggling with herself. Maybe she was seeing the face of her husband, whom she would see again shortly. I think that at the end of life, everybody knows that, feels that.

I sensed that I was losing her. She would just sit by the window and gaze out. What could she have seen from her armchair? She kept her hands in her lap, those old person hands. I felt as if I had not been aware of their age until then, or if I had, I would have looked, scared and

115

instinctively, at my own hands. Old age had left its traces, namely some brown spots.

"Yes, she will die soon," I told myself, leaving the room. "She doesn't want to live anymore. Charles, that King whom she loved, will he wait for her? I wonder. Is she thinking of him?" She talked very little, so I could not possibly have found that out. I, too, had become more introverted.

The inevitable occurred in November, the month of her birthday, when she did not get out of bed. Two nuns and I were taking care of her, but she always made that sign for me to leave, whispering to me "Go and get some sleep!" The nuns were watching and gestured that they would look after her so I could go to my room. That situation was awkward, for I had been there by her side all my life, and now I was the one being sent to sleep, as if I were able to do that. But I could not fight it. This went on for a whole month.

She called to see me on Christmas, and she waved at the two women for them to leave. She pointed with her gaunt hand, which frightened me, to the chest between the two windows. I went to it and opened the top drawer, as I understood from her gestures. There were her jewels from Charles. She indicated that I should take them all.

"It's a present!" she whispered, "Nobody knows about them!" she went on. I knelt down and cried with my head in the bed clothes. She caressed my gray hair and let me collect myself. Then I understood, with difficulty, that she had had the same dream as in the summer and that she knew her ending was near. I understood that I had to convince Pedro and the others in the family come and see her. I told her all that, and she understood. Then I left, taking the jewels that would, in a way, stand in for her in the future. The nuns were by the door, and I ordered them to get a priest, who was nearby in that lovely chapel of Bemposta.

"I am going to the palace," I told them, and they made the sign of the cross, one entering Catarina's room and the other running to the chapel.

I remember the weather then. It was raining as it had never rained before. I reached the palace, where the guards let me pass immediately. I asked to see the King, and he was frightened by my appearance.

"Your Majesty's sister sent me! She is dying and she wants to say goodbye."

The King was afraid, but then composed himself and ordered that all the children be prepared. He loved his sister, and one could see that. He dismissed me, leaving me with a servant, who gave me hot tea. We left then in two coaches to Bemposta.

We all entered at the same time, and Catarina reminded me about the letter, simply by lifting her hand. I went out quickly, and came back with the letter. When she saw me, she composed herself and closed her eyes. She had died. And I had to read what she had written in front of everybody. Her love overflowed from every word I read, and I cried a river. She died being mourned by everybody.

From England, we received only a detached, formal letter from Anne, in a diplomatic, typical tone, whereby she expressed her condolences for the death of her aunt. Pedro was only a shadow compared to his son Joao. No one, in that moment could have foreseen that one year later, the King would sleep his eternal sleep, just like his sister. Pedro was paler and more tired than ever. He was 57, and looked as if he were 80. He asked me to stay in Bemposta Palace until after the funeral, and then I could move into my house, but all by myself that time.

Accompanied on her last journey by us and the members of the Court, Catarina was acclaimed by the Portuguese from everywhere, in all the streets. She was the daughter of the man who had brought Portugal back from the Spanish, she was a martyr for religion, she was priceless. But, above it all, she had been my friend, who had always understood me, who had listened to me, and thanks to whom I had known the love of Gaspar Juan. She had been my idol in life; she had been the building, and I was the ivy clinging onto her, thus being tightly united.

After that sad event, I spent one more week in Bemposta, during which I covered everything in the house and made all the necessary arrangements, so that everything would stay intact and not deteriorate, and then I left for home.

EPILOGUE

I am writing with my hand on the chains at my neck. I am older than death, which will not take me. I have buried my brothers and their wives. I have left only a few kind nephews, who behave and open the door for me. I live and they keep up with me.

When Pedro II died, I was next to him like his sister's shadow. I attended the coronation of Joao at a very young age, most unusual, at seventeen. But what impressed me more was the wedding in 1708 between Joao V and his cousin, Maria Anne of Austria, who was six years older than he. I was envious, old as I was. All my life I have dedicated myself to others, forgetting about myself. I had never been a bride – maybe only to Christ. But I should stop thinking wrongly; I chose that path.

I came back to my home, where I sit and watch the flowers in the garden. They are beautiful, too, and then they fade. I couldn't stay in Bemposta anymore, even if the young King had asked me to on his knees. Sometimes I wake up looking at the painting of Gaspar Juan. We were two unhappy people. He was more fortunate because he died young. I wondered if the ivy had spread onto the graves of the dukes of Medina Sidonia. I had an annuity from Pedro's son, which I received on a regular basis, because I was something of a relic, a dinosaur of his family.

Sometimes I would write to Maria de Modena in France, but when I learned that her daughter had passed away, I swore not to hear of dead people anymore, and I never wrote back. I am waiting for my own eternity. I am tired of hearing about other people leaving this world.

It is 1713, and I have decided not to write anymore. I do not have anything or anybody to write about. All my generation is gone, I am the only one left, so as to set an example of survival. I am 72, I'm still standing and walking on my feet; my teeth are still amazingly good. I eat, I do well, but I refuse to see any more doctors. For certain I shall live forever. Someone has forgotten me down here on earth.

As long as Catarina lived, I had a purpose, that of serving her, of being by her side. But now I have no purpose. Goodbye.

Juliana de Alfambra

"No one has forgotten you, aunt, down here! You extinguished like a candle, ten years later. In 1723. Even the younger Maria de Modena died before you. You lived for 82 years, and you are sleeping now in the burial chamber of the Earls of Alfambra. We thank you for having lived and for having left this enchanting manuscript. You did not live for nothing, for we who are still alive have learned so much from you.

I almost forgot. My daughter is living in your house now, and when we buried you, we let you go together with the letters from your duke and the jewels as well as your memories, and Manuela, my daughter, removed the frame from the painting, and put the canvas into your coffin. So you do have your duke with you now!

Miguel of Alfambra
1724"

THE END

The following novels written by the same author were published also by Infarom Publishing:

"*Destine*" *(Destinies);*
"*Lucia; Tatăl meu este soarele şi mama mea este luna*" *(Lucia; My father is the sun, and my mother is the moon);*
"*Once I was King*".